Harlequin Romance®
presents
an exciting new duet by
international bestselling author

LUCY GORDON

Italian Brothers

Where there's a will, there's a wedding!

Rinaldo and Gino Farnese are wealthy,
proud, passionate brothers who live in the
heart of Tuscany, Italy. Their late father's will brings
one surprise that ultimately leads to two more—
a bride for each of them!

Book 1: *Rinaldo's Inherited Bride* #3799
Book 2: *Gino's Arranged Bride* #3807

Dear Reader,

In *Gino's Arranged Bride* we once more meet Gino Farnese, the laughing charmer of *Rinaldo's Inherited Bride*. But now everything in his world is different.

The lighthearted boy has gone. In his place is a bitter, despairing man, banished from his home by his unrequited love for his brother's wife, and certain that he will never love or be happy again.

Drifting from country to country, haunted by Alex, he comes to England, where he meets Laura and her little girl, Nikki, and his generous heart is drawn to them by their need.

Nikki, who has a mild facial disfigurement, sees in him a father to replace the one who rejected her. Laura, her mother, is struggling to scrape a living and keep her daughter's spirits up.

In devoting himself to their service, Gino finds a new reason for living. He even accepts Laura's suggestion of marriage, for Nikki's sake. It's a far cry from his violent passion for Alex, but it's contentment of a kind, and he reckons it will have to do.

But Laura won't settle for second best. She knows that only in Tuscany will Gino find the answers he is still seeking. Yet returning to Tuscany means meeting Alex, the woman who still reigns in his heart. Laura fears Alex most of all, but until she faces her—and Gino faces her—she knows that he will never be truly hers.

Best wishes,

Lucy Gordon

GINO'S ARRANGED BRIDE

Lucy Gordon

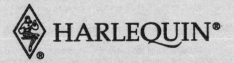

TORONTO • NEW YORK • LONDON
AMSTERDAM • PARIS • SYDNEY • HAMBURG
STOCKHOLM • ATHENS • TOKYO • MILAN • MADRID
PRAGUE • WARSAW • BUDAPEST • AUCKLAND

ISBN 0-373-03807-0

GINO'S ARRANGED BRIDE

First North American Publication 2004.

CHAPTER ONE

ONE of the most beautiful men Nature ever made, Laura thought appreciatively. *And I don't just mean good-looking. Beautiful!*

The young man leaning back on the park bench would have caught anyone's attention. His shaggy dark hair was just beginning to curl. His features were lean and fine, except for his mouth which was wide and generous, sensually curved even when he was asleep.

There wasn't a spare ounce on his tall body with its long legs, stretched out gracefully. An old jacket, worn jeans, and a day's growth on his chin, made him look like a hobo, but a stylish hobo.

With his eyes closed, his face raised to the sun, he might have stood for a pagan symbol of physical perfection.

He's probably got nothing between his ears, she thought, amused, *but with looks like that, he doesn't need it.*

But then she thought again. There was something in his face that told another story. Heavy shadows beneath his eyes, and a fine-drawn tension about his mouth suggested a man who lived on his nerves, and who hadn't slept properly for months.

'Mummy.'

Laura turned to where her eight-year-old daughter was standing beside her, clutching a football, eagerly waiting for the fun to begin.

'Sorry, darling,' she said, turning away from the man on the bench.

'Please let's play a game, Mummy.'

On the first real day of spring Nikki had wanted to get out of the house and celebrate in the park. Laura had protested at first.

'It's not really warm enough yet.'

'It is, it *is*,' Nikki had insisted indignantly.

And it was. The weather was lovely. But Laura had another reason for being reluctant to face the world, one that she couldn't put into words for the little girl, although Nikki understood without words.

Before leaving the house she had run a brush through her fair, generous curls that rioted in disorder no matter how she tried to control them. Her appearance told two different stories. Her hair seemed to belong to a cheerful, careless teenager, and at thirty-two she still had the slim figure of those years.

But her face had been shaped by sadness and weary patience. It was too soon for lines, but a shadow had come into her blue eyes years too soon.

What devastated her was that the same shadow was beginning to appear in her daughter's eyes. At eight, Nikki was already losing her childish light-heartedness, for a terrible reason. And there was nothing her frantic mother could do about it.

The park was already filling up. Children were kicking balls about, adults were leaning back in the sun.

Laura recognised some of the other mothers and waved to them. They waved back, but then turned away quickly. She glanced quickly at Nikki to see if she had noticed the rejection, and found her daughter regarding her with an understanding smile.

'It's all right,' she said in a confiding voice. 'We'll play together.'

At such moments Laura wanted to scream to the world, *'How dare you reject my daughter? So what if her face is a little different? What harm does it do you?'*

But Nikki was already darting away, deftly dribbling the ball between her feet. She seemed to have put the incident behind her.

If only I could do that, Laura thought. *If only I could still believe the world will turn out to be a good place in the end, as she does.*

She took a last glimpse at the glorious young man, still sitting motionless, bathed in the sun.

Not that Laura set much store by looks. Jack, too, had been handsome, with a broad, good-natured smile and an air of loving the world—until the day he walked out on his wife and daughter without a backward glance.

Nikki was still playing with her junior football, which she bounced hopefully, looking around her.

'I don't see anyone that we know, darling,' Laura said. 'Let's just play together.'

'You mean they wouldn't want to play with me?' Nikki asked.

Laura's heart lurched, and her eyes reacted before she could stop herself. Nikki watched and understood.

'It's all right, Mummy.' The little girl rubbed her face. 'People don't understand about this.'

'No, they don't understand,' Laura said gently.

'Was that why you didn't want us to come here?'

Dear God! Laura thought. She's only eight years old. She knows far too much.

She nodded. 'Yes, because of people who don't understand, being unkind to you.'

'They're not unkind *exactly*,' Nikki said, speaking like a wise little old woman, 'it's just that they don't like to look at me. Never mind.'

She ran a little distance ahead and began dribbling the ball, while Laura stood still for a moment, suppressing the instinct to commit murder.

But murder who? The malign fate that had caused her child to be different to others? The stupid world that made everything worse for her with its cruel, imbecilic ignorance? The unthinking idiots who couldn't see past that damaged face to the sweet loving soul beneath.

'Come on, Mummy,' Nikki called.

They kicked the football around for a while, until Nikki gave an unexpectedly powerful lunge and the ball went sailing high in the air.

For a moment it seemed to hover before plunging like a stone to land right on the stomach of the young man on the bench. He awoke with a yell, clutching his middle.

Nikki had run forward until she pulled up short in front of him and stood looking at him steadily.

He looked back at her. He was holding the ball.

'This is yours?' he asked. He had a foreign accent.

'Yes. Sorry.' Nikki moved closer, positioning herself just in front of him, so that he couldn't help but see her clearly. Her eyes were fixed on his face, watching, waiting for the moment when his glance faltered.

Where does she get the courage to do that? Laura wondered.

'I hope you really are sorry,' he said, regarding her steadily and speaking in a tone of grievance. 'I was enjoying a beautiful dream when Poof! There is a dead weight on my stomach.'

He hadn't reacted to her face. Nikki moved again,

placing herself squarely before him, grimly determined, daring her good luck not to last.

'I didn't mean to,' she said.

'Of course not.'

'I do apologise,' Laura said, catching up with them. 'I hope you're not hurt.'

He gave them both a brilliant grin that seemed to light up the whole world. Laura had never seen a grin like it. It was life enhancing.

'I guess I'll survive,' he said.

'And it's left a dirty patch in your shirt.'

He studied the shirt which was already the worse for wear. 'How can you tell?' he asked plaintively.

Nikki giggled. He directed his grin at her.

Laura watched him carefully, wondering if this was really happening. Other people flinched at the sight of Nikki, or became elaborately kind, which was almost worse. This man seemed not to have noticed anything different about her.

'I'm Laura Gray,' she said, 'and this is my daughter, Nikki.'

'I'm Gino Farnese.' He engulfed her hand in his. It was a big hand with a powerful, muscular look that suggested some kind of hard manual work. Even through the gentle handshake she could feel the strength.

Then he grasped Nikki's hand, giving her the same courtesy as her mother, and saying solemnly, *'Buon giorno, signorina. Sono Gino.'*

'What does that mean?' the child asked.

'It means, "Hello, young lady. I am Gino."'

Nikki frowned. 'You're foreign,' she declared bluntly. 'You talk funny.'

'Nikki!' Laura exclaimed. 'Manners!'

'It's true. I'm Italian,' he said, not seeming to be offended.

'Are you any good kicking a football?' Nikki demanded, keeping him to important matters.

'*Nikki!*'

'I reckon I'm pretty useful,' he said, adding warily, 'as long as my opponent doesn't get too rough.'

She bounded away, calling to him, 'Come on, come *on*!'

'I apologise,' Laura said helplessly.

He gave his life-enhancing grin again. 'Don't worry. I'm on my guard against further assaults from your ferocious offspring.'

'That wasn't what I—'

But he was gone, dancing around the ball. He really was skilled, Laura thought. Not every man could have kicked it here and there, never too hard, just far enough to make her work for it. And it all looked natural.

Smiling, Laura took his place on the bench, almost tripping over a suitcase that stood beside it.

It was shabby, like the rest of him. His clothes looked as though he'd spent several nights sleeping in them, and the suitcase had a hole in the corner.

Like a tortoise, she thought, carrying everything on its back. Not that there was anything tortoise-like about the deft way he was darting back and forth.

At last he contrived to lose the ball to Nikki so cleverly that she could think she'd won it. She promptly gave it another of her mighty kicks straight at him. Gino Farnese lunged like a goalkeeper, just contriving to miss.

'*Goal!*' he yelled triumphantly, sitting on the ground, and bawling so loudly that several people stared at him and moved hastily away.

'That always happens,' he said. 'People run away from me because they think I'm crazy.'

'Are you crazy?' Nikki wanted to know.

He seemed to consider. 'I think so, *si*. So you can't blame them.'

'I won't run away,' Nikki said.

'Thank you.' He was still sitting on the ground, gasping, looking her in the eyes. 'Oh, I can't do this, *piccina*. You're too much for me.'

He jumped up and went off to retrieve the ball. Nikki darted to her mother and spoke in a hurried whisper.

'He didn't see it, Mummy. He didn't see it.'

'Darling—'

'It's like a magic spell. Everyone else can see it but not him. Do you think there's really a spell on me?'

With all her heart she longed to say yes. She was saved from having to answer by Gino's return. She came to a swift decision.

'It's time we were going back to have some tea,' she said. 'I hope you'll come with us. The least I can do is feed you when my daughter has run you off your feet.'

'That's very kind—'

'Fine, then you're coming.' She wasn't going to let him escape. 'The house is just over there. Besides, I don't think Nikki is ready to let you go yet.'

She was right. The little girl was hopping excitedly from one foot to the other. Laura could see that she'd formed one of those instant, inexplicable friendships that sometimes happened with children.

Or was it inexplicable? He'd treated her exactly like any other child, which was all Nikki asked. No, not inexplicable at all.

The little girl danced beside him all the way home, chattering, giggling at his accent. He promptly exaggerated it, making her giggle more. Laura gave him full marks for a kind heart.

Her home was a huge three-storey Victorian house with a shabby appearance, although inwardly it was clean and comfortable in a 'no frills' kind of way.

'You two live here alone?' he asked.

'No, I rent out rooms.'

'Ah! Are you expensive?'

'Not very. In fact my only remaining room is smaller than the others and always the last to go, so it's dirt cheap.'

She hoped she didn't sound too eager. She had made her own decision as firmly as Nikki had apparently made hers. She wanted him to move in as a tenant, and make her little girl smile.

The front door led into a wide hallway, with a flight of stairs on one side and a door on the other.

'That's the living room,' Laura said, pushing it open. 'It's got the only television in the house. This place is as basic as that, I'm afraid. And along here, at the back of the house, is the kitchen.'

It was old-fashioned, large and comfortable, with a large table in the centre. Of the six chairs around it only three of them matched.

As Laura put the kettle on Gino Farnese said, 'You should know something about me before you let me come here.'

Nikki was putting her ball away in the hall cupboard, and Laura took the chance to say quietly, 'I know that you can cheer her up. That's important.'

'But it's not the only thing,' he said, also dropping his voice. 'To make a little girl smile—is important, *si*. But you don't know me. I might have married six wives and abandoned them all.'

'You're a bit young to have married six wives,' she said, apparently considering the matter seriously. 'You can't be much more than twenty-five.'

'Twenty-nine,' he said with wounded dignity.

'I'm sorry, twenty-nine. So tell me, *have* you abandoned six wives?'

'No, no, only four—no, five,' he assured her quickly. 'It's not so bad, *si*?'

A giggle from the door told them Nikki had been eavesdropping.

'Five's all right, isn't it Mummy.'

'I suppose we can overlook five,' she agreed, laughing.

'But when I said you should know about me, that's not when I meant,' he told her. 'I must tell you that I have hardly any money at the moment. I was—er—' he struck his forehead while he fought for the English word '*come si dice?*—I was mugged.'

'Goodness, when?'

'In London. I don't like London. It's too big and noisy. Three of them jumped me, grabbed my bags and ran. I didn't even get a good look at them.

'Luckily I had my passport and a little money in my back pocket, but my wallet with credit cards was in one of the bags. So were my decent clothes.'

'Did you go to the police?'

'Sure, but what can they do? I've cancelled the credit cards, but now I must get some more money. I bought some old clothes in a charity shop, also an old suitcase. Now I wear the old clothes so that my good suit stays in the bag.

'I had just enough money to get a train out of London, to anywhere. I just got off here because it looked nice, a small town, some countryside. But I don't know where I am. The station board said Elverham, but where is Elverham? What is Elverham? Is it real, or did I imagine it?'

He saw her looking at him and came down to earth.

'I'm sorry. I warned you I'm a little crazy.'

'I guess you're entitled to be. Elverham is about sixty miles north of London, and it's a market town, surrounded by country. It's a quiet place. Nothing very dramatic ever happens here. So you got off the train and did what?'

'I wandered about and found the park. It looked nice so I lay down under a bush and stayed the night. That's why I look a bit—well—' His gesture indicated his dishevelled appearance.

Nikki beamed, evidently not liking him less for looking like a tramp.

'Tomorrow I'll try to open a bank account and get some money sent from Italy,' he said. 'Until then I have almost nothing, so if you want a deposit for the room I can't do it today, I'm afraid.'

'There's no rush. You should try the room out first. You may not like it.'

'After the way I slept last night, I'll like it,' he assured her, and they all laughed.

'I've done Italy in geography,' Nikki said proudly. 'It looks like a boot. Which bit do you come from?'

She thought he hesitated a moment before replying, 'Tuscany.'

Nikki frowned. 'Where's that?'

'When you look at the map, it's the bit on the left, near the top,' he explained.

'And that's where your home is?' Nikki persisted.

The question seemed to trouble him. His expression

became a little vague, and he murmured, 'My home,' in an almost inaudible voice.

'Yes, you know, a place where they have to let you in, even if they don't like you.'

'Nikki,' Laura groaned again.

'It's not a bad description,' Gino said with a faint smile. 'Yes, there's a place where they'd have to let me in.'

'Is it like this?' Nikki wanted to know.

He laughed outright. 'No, it's a farm.'

'Is it big?'

'Too big. Too much work. I just ran away. Something smells good.'

'It's only a cup of tea,' Laura pointed out. 'I'll pour you one.'

Laura did so, appreciating the neat way he'd slid away from the subject of his home. She wondered exactly what he was running from. Not hard work, as he'd implied. But he was escaping something. There had been an odd look on his face, that hinted at troubled currents beneath.

She wasn't sure how much of this robbery story she believed. It might just be his way of saying that he wasn't really a vagrant, no matter how things looked.

An instinctive clown, she thought, but one who clowned as a way of hiding himself.

If it came to that, she supposed it was true that she knew nothing about him. He might be all kinds of a weirdo.

But then she looked at him, and calculations fell away. This was a good man. All her instincts told her so.

'I'll get your room ready,' she said.

He followed her up the stairs to the next floor where

three of the rented rooms were located, the other two being on the floor above. She led him to the one at the far end of the corridor, with Nikki bringing up the rear.

As Laura had warned him, it was tiny. The bed was narrow and only just long enough for his tall figure. There was a wardrobe, a chest of drawers, a chair and a small washbasin attached to the wall.

Even so, he had space enough for his meagre possessions.

Laura fetched sheets and blankets and began making up the bed with Nikki's help, so that Gino had to hop out of the way in that narrow space.

'Can't I do anything useful?' he asked.

'You could put the pillow in its case,' Nikki told him kindly.

'Thank you ma'am.'

As they worked Laura said, 'I have five other guests. Sadie and Claudia are sisters, and they both work at making computers in a local factory. Bert is a night-watchman, Fred is a bouncer at a nightclub, and Mrs Baxter is a widow and retired teacher. She keeps an eye on Nikki when I have to work in the evening.'

'You work, as well as running this place?' he asked, startled.

'I do a few hours as a barmaid. The pub's not far away.'

When it was all finished they stood back and regarded the result.

'I'm afraid it's a bit bare,' Laura said.

'I know what we can do,' Nikki said. She disappeared and returned a moment later, clutching something that she laid triumphantly on the little chest of drawers by the bed.

It was a small soft toy in the shape of a dog.

'His name's Simon,' she said. 'And he'll keep you company.'

Gino sat down on the bed so that his eyes were on a level with hers.

'Thank you,' he said gravely. 'That was very kind. Now I shall have a friend.'

'Three friends,' Nikki said at once. ''Cos you've got us too.'

He raised his eyes to Laura, signalling a question.

'Yes, you've got three friends now,' she agreed. 'I've got to go and start the supper. Come along Nikki. If Gino slept on the ground last night he's probably longing to get some sleep now.'

He smiled and didn't deny it.

When they had left he threw himself back on the bed and lay looking at the ceiling, waiting for sleep to come. After the uncomfortable night he'd had, it should happen easily.

But, as he'd feared, there was only restless wakefulness. By now he was drearily used to that happening. Once he'd been a man who slept easily, like a contented animal, living through his happy physical instincts.

But in the six months since he'd left Italy that had all changed. Now it seemed that he rested properly only one night out of two. The others were spent in chasing wretched dreams and visions, wrestling with regrets and 'if onlys'.

The child's mention of 'home' had caught him off guard, as so many things seemed to do these days.

'A place where they have to let you in, even if they don't like you.'

Home was Belluna, the great farm in Tuscany. If he knocked on the door, his brother and Alex, his brother's wife—for so he must force himself to call her now—

would let him in. They would have to, since he owned half the property.

They would smile and say how good it was to see him, how concerned they'd been while he was away, how they'd thought about him every day.

And it would all be true.

But there was something else, also true, that nobody would mention. They would worry, lest he rock the boat of their happy marriage with his bitterness and anger, his anguished, unrequited love. They would look at each other behind his back, and know that an alien had come among them. And they would long silently for him to leave.

'I could never love you,' Alex had said. 'Not as you want, anyway.'

But even she had never understood how deeply in love with her he had fallen. Before that he'd loved as a very young man, plunging into infatuation and out again, like the giddy whirl of a carousel.

But when he met Alex the carousel had stopped, tossing him to the ground so that he rose into a new world, one where *she* existed. The one. The only one, for, like many young men who love lightly and carelessly, he had been struck by the real thing like a thunderbolt. After that no more carelessness was possible.

'Not as you want,' she had said.

He had wanted everything from her, love, tenderness, passion, a promise to last a lifetime.

And he'd thought he had them, until the night he returned to find her in his brother's bed.

CHAPTER TWO

SOMETIMES the dreams were worse than the waking memories. If you were awake you could decide not to think about it, but dreams were remorseless.

In dreams he had no choice but to live again the moment at the Belluna harvest party where he'd told Alex of his love in front of all their neighbours.

Even now his own words and actions could give him a shiver of shame.

'You've always known how I felt about you,' he'd said with all the force of his love. 'Even when I was playing the fool, my heart was all yours.'

Then he'd gone down on one knee, in the sight of them all, and begged her to be his wife.

Even when she'd looked at him in dismay he hadn't understood, so deeply submerged was he in his own illusion.

He'd thought she was just embarrassed at receiving a proposal in public, and when they were alone a few minutes later he'd been sure that all would be well. Driven by his overwhelming feelings, he'd told her passionately that she was the one.

'The *only* one, different from every other woman I've fooled around with and loved for five minutes. It's not five minutes this time, but all my life and beyond—'

She'd stopped him there, telling him kindly but plainly that she did not love him. Still he couldn't, *wouldn't* believe it, because it was too monstrous to be

19

true. So he'd left, telling himself that he would be back later, and make her understand.

Fool! *Fool!*

He awoke with a start, sitting up in bed, shaking.

It was dark, and from down below he could hear the murmur of voices. He got out of bed and went to the window, where the turn of the house showed him the lit window of the kitchen, and moving shadows beyond.

The others must have returned, but he couldn't go down and meet them now. He knew, from experience, that what was happening inside his head couldn't be stopped. Once he'd started down this bitter path it must be walked to the end. But he would have avoided the next stage if he could.

He'd fled the party, staying away into the early hours, then returning home. There he would seek out Rinaldo, the brother who'd been like a second father to him. Rinaldo, the man he trusted above all others, would know how to advise him.

Dawn was breaking when he went to Rinaldo's room and walked in without knocking.

What he saw stopped him like a blow. Alex was in the bed, lying on her back, her eyes closed, breathing evenly. And there with her was Rinaldo, sleeping against her chest, wrapped in the protective curve of her arms. The sheet was thrown right back, revealing that they were both completely naked.

He had dreamed of seeing her naked body, but not like this, embracing his brother in the peace that follows passion.

She had awoken first, her face full of horror as she saw him there in the faint light of dawn. Her lips framed his name, she reached out a hand to him, but he backed away as though her touch would kill him.

From the scene that had followed he recalled only the cruel discovery that these two had escaped into another world, one from which he was excluded. Rinaldo had said sadly but firmly, 'I didn't take her from you. The choice was hers.'

It was true. Alex hadn't deceived him. He'd deceived himself. She was not to blame. He kept telling himself that because he needed to keep her on her pedestal. However painful it was, it hurt less than blaming her.

He knew they didn't understand how the world had shattered around him. Because he had laughed his way through life they'd thought he would laugh this off too. He'd had so many girls. What did it matter if he lost one?

Only he knew that she had been 'the one', and always would be, as long as he lived. Her loss was a catastrophe that shook him to the soul, driving him away so that he would not have to see them together.

In losing Alex he had also lost his home. For six months he had travelled, anywhere, as long as it was away from Belluna. As part owner he was entitled to draw an income from the farm, but he drew as little as possible, conscious that he was not there to help with the work.

He took any job he could get, preferably hard manual labour so that he could tire himself out. In this way he earned just enough to get by, until he could decide what he wanted to do. But he could not settle, and he travelled on, always trying to avoid her face, always seeing it dance before him. In the end he had come to England, Alex's country, where he was always bound to finish.

Now he seemed to have reached a place that was largely featureless. Despite what Laura had told him he had no real idea where the town was in relation to the rest of England and the rest of the world. And in an odd way that suited him.

He had come to nowhere, and he had nothing. When he'd been to the bank he would possess a little money, but he would still, in all important senses, have nothing.

He was cut adrift from his family and everything he knew, and he had no way of going home, because home no longer existed.

Gino opened his eyes to darkness. He must have slept again after all, so deeply that evening had passed into night. His watch told him it was nearly midnight.

He rose, feeling strangely well rested after his turbulent sleep. Looking into the corridor he saw that the rest of the house was dark and quiet.

The other guests must have returned, eaten and gone to bed, shutting their doors. He could see some of those doors in the gloom, all alike.

Which one was the bathroom? How did a stranger find out? Try each one? Hell!

To his relief he heard the front door open and looked over the stair rail to see Laura coming in.

'Psst!' he said urgently. *'Aiuto!'*

'Pardon?'

'Help. T'imploro!'

'Why, what's the matter?'

'I need—' in his panic his English deserted him. *'Un gabinetto,'* he said. *'Ti prego—ti prego, un gabinetto.'*

Laura knew no Italian but she guessed the frantic note in his voice was the same in every language.

'Here,' she said, opening a door under the stairs.

'Grazie, grazie!'

He leapt down the stairs three at a time, shot into the tiny bathroom, and she heard the lock. Grinning in sympathy she slipped upstairs to check Nikki, who was asleep. As she returned to the kitchen and put on the kettle, Gino emerged looking a lot happier.

'Thank you,' he said fervently. 'I'm sorry I shouted at you in Italian. *Gabinetto* means—'

'I think I have a pretty good idea of what it means by now,' she said, and they both laughed.

The kettle boiled, but when she turned to it he stopped her.

'You sit down,' he said. 'I make the tea. You must be very tired.'

'Thanks.' She flopped gratefully into a chair. 'Do you know how to make English tea?'

'I watched you this afternoon. There, did I do it right?'

The tea was delicious.

'How many evenings do you work behind a bar?' he wanted to know.

'Three, usually.'

'On top of running this place? When do you have a life?'

'Nikki is my life. Nothing else matters.'

'And you are alone?' he asked delicately.

'You mean, do I have a husband? I did have. We were very happy, until Nikki was four years old. She adored Jack and he seemed to adore her. Anyone seeing them together would have said he was the perfect father.

'Then something happened to her face. It began to grow too much, and in ways that it shouldn't. You can see that her forehead is too large. And Jack left. He just upped and left.'

'*Maria Vergine!*' he exclaimed softly. '*Un criminale!*'

'If that means what I think it does, yes.'

'And the *piccina*, how much does she know?'

'She knows that her father rejected her. She pretends not to, for my sake. But she knows.'

'But is there no cure?'

'Eventually they might be able to do some surgery that puts things right. But not now, while her bones are still growing. In the meantime, she has to wait and suffer. People can be so cruel. They think because she looks different she must be stupid.'

'No, no, she's a very bright little girl.'

'I know, but they tell their children not to play with her. Sometimes they try to be "nice", but there's something self-conscious about it, as though they're congratulating themselves on how nice they're being.'

'How does she manage at school?'

'She's got a few good friends, and most of the teachers are decent. But some of the other kids bully and tease her, and one teacher actually dared to tell me I should take her out of school because she "couldn't fit in". She said Nikki needed a place for children with special needs.'

Gino swore softly.

'I told her the only special need Nikki had was to be treated with intelligence and understanding. Then I complained to the headmistress, who, luckily, is one of the good guys, and I didn't have any more trouble from that teacher. But there are always plenty more where she came from.

'With luck, Nikki will be all right one day. But by that time she'll have been through all these experiences.'

'And what happens to her now will mark her for life,' he said, nodding.

'You made her so happy in the park today, because

you didn't seem to notice. You looked straight at her and didn't register anything—not shock, or surprise, nothing. It was—oh, I can't tell you how wonderful it was, and what it meant to her.'

Gino concentrated on his tea, hoping that his unease didn't show in his face. He was guiltily aware that he did not deserve her praise. The fact was that he'd been too wrapped up in himself and his own troubles that morning to be aware of anything else.

Laura was still talking eagerly.

'She's got this theory that someone must have cast a magic spell, so that you didn't really see her face.'

'In a way she's right,' he said. 'But the spell was my own self-absorption. I was so busy feeling sorry for myself that I actually didn't see her for several moments, even though I was looking at her. So I haven't earned your kindness.'

'But don't you see, that doesn't matter? You made her happy without even knowing. So maybe she's right, and it really was a magic spell.'

He nodded. 'Who cares about the reason if it gave her what she needed? Her face doesn't matter. She's a lovely child.'

'Yes, she is,' Laura said eagerly. 'But all she sees is what she reads in the eyes of other people.'

'I promise you, she'll never suffer from what she sees in my eyes,' Gino said seriously.

'Thank you. You have no idea how important that is.'

Next day at breakfast he met some of the other boarders. Sadie and Claudia, the sisters, were quiet, thin and middle-aged. Their lives revolved around computers, and they could launch into a discussion of the latest technology at the drop of a hat. They worked in Compulor, a nearby computer factory, where they both held positions of responsibility.

Mrs Baxter was the eldest, a bright-eyed little bird of a woman, who looked Gino up and down, and gave a grunt which seemed to imply approval.

Sadie and Claudia were also friendly.

'We've been to Italy,' Sadie confided.

'There was a very interesting computer fair in Milan,' Claudia added. 'Do you know Milan, Signor Farnese?'

'Gino, please,' he said at once. 'No, I've never been to Milan. Tuscany is my part of the world.'

They were full of intelligent questions about Tuscany which Gino answered courteously but reluctantly. He didn't want to dwell on his home just now.

'We don't usually see Bert and Fred at breakfast,' Laura explained. 'Fred doesn't come home until the nightclub has closed in the early hours. Bert is a nightwatchman, so he got in five minutes ago and went straight to bed.'

Nikki set off for school accompanied by Mrs Baxter who, although retired, occasionally worked there parttime. Before she left, Nikki addressed Gino like a perfect hostess, 'I'm afraid I have to go now, but I'll be back later.'

'I'll look forward to that,' he told her solemnly.

He helped Laura with the washing up, surprising her with his efficiency.

'I thought Italian men were old-fashioned and macho,' she said. 'Working in the kitchen is for women, that kind of thing.'

'You do us wrong, we're very domesticated. When I was a little boy my mother taught me how to do these things, ''just in case you ever have to'', was how she put it. She showed me how to wash a cup, and when I'd finished she said, ''All right, now you know how to do it, go and play''.'

'And that was it?'

'That was my domestic education. But I must say this for myself—I wash a mean cup.'

They laughed together and finished putting things away.

She drove him into town in her little car, and they managed to get to see the bank manager after only a short wait.

'It'll take a few days for funds to arrive from your Italian account to your new one with us,' the manager said. 'But in the meantime there'll be no problem if you overdraw a little.'

Gino's first action was to pay Laura two weeks' rent.

'For this week and next,' he said.

'But this week's almost over,' she protested.

'Business is business. Half a week counts as a full week.'

'I'm the landlady. Shouldn't I be the one saying that?'

'You should, but you're a terrible businesswoman, so I'm saying it for you.' He looked at her kindly. 'Someone needs to look out for you.'

It was so long since anyone had looked out for her that at first the words were almost startling.

'I still feel guilty taking this,' she said.

'Don't worry, you'll earn it. I'll be the most trouble-some tenant you've ever had.'

By way of demonstrating just how awkward he could be he came round the shops with her, carrying things and generally making himself useful, explaining that he was improving his English

Sometimes he clowned, claiming not to know words that she was sure he did know. He would throw himself on her mercy with a piteous air that made her laugh.

Gradually she absorbed the message that he was sending out. She could relax. He was harmless. All he asked was to be left in peace to wrestle with whatever demons were driving him.

Laura was happy to give him the space he needed, but she was curious about him. Although he talked a lot, most of his words were the equivalent of blowing bubbles in the air. The amount of real information he disclosed about himself was almost nil.

She, on the other hand, found herself revealing more than she could remember ever doing.

'I was born around here,' she told him as they sat over tea and toast when they stopped for a break. 'And I thought this was the dullest place on earth. I wanted London and the bright lights.'

'Did you ever manage it?'

'Yes, I enrolled in a London dance academy. I was in the chorus of a few shows. Then six of us got together and formed a little dance troupe. Jack was our agent.'

'Sounds like a match made in heaven. Did he try to make you a star?'

She laughed ruefully. 'No. I did hope about that for a while, but once we were married he wanted me to give it all up and be domestic.

'We argued about it for a while, but then I found I was pregnant. And when Nikki came along I just wanted to be with her. Besides, I'd put on a few pounds that I've never managed to shift since.'

He surveyed her critically. 'I can't see them.'

'They're still there, and they're just too much for me to be a dancer. Anyway, I'm too old now.'

'Eighty?' he hazarded. 'Ninety?'

'Thirty-two.'

'You're kidding. You don't look a day over fifty.'

She laughed, but there was a shadow in her manner, and he was immediately contrite.

'I'm sorry, that wasn't funny.'

'No, I'm just being over-sensitive. It was a mistake for me to start talking about the past. It reminded me that I promised myself that by the time I was thirty my name would be in lights.'

'Don't you talk about the past normally?'

'Who with? Not Nikki, it would be too painful for her. And why would the tenants be interested? They come and go.'

He had a sudden vivid picture of her isolation, the burdens she was carrying alone.

'Did you come back to live here after you broke up with your husband?' he asked.

'Yes, I couldn't have stayed in London. For one thing it was too expensive, and for another he—well, I suppose he bribed me to go away. He was becoming fairly well known in showbiz. He didn't want to risk the ''beautiful people'' learning that he had a daughter who wasn't perfect. He said it would hurt him professionally.

'So he offered me a better settlement to get out, and I accepted it because that was best for Nikki anyway. I came back here and used the money to buy the house. It's a living.'

'Not much of one if you have to work in the evenings too. When do you sleep?'

'Ah, but look on the bright side. I never have to pay

for babysitting. There's always someone at home with Nikki, and she likes them all.'

'So none of them reacted hurtfully to her face?'

'No, but I warned them all before they saw her. I never leave it to chance, if I can help it, and of course she guesses that. It's people like you she values, the ones who had no warning.'

'I just hope I don't let her down.'

Laura frowned. 'I don't think that's possible,' she said thoughtfully. 'It's the spell, you see. It's cast over you too, and whatever you do, she'll see it in the best way, in the light of that spell.'

'You talk as though you believe in magic,' he said curiously.

'If someone is determined to think the best of you, no matter what you do, I think that a kind of magic spell.'

The words gave him a strange feeling, as if she'd looked into his mind. Only last night he'd known that he had to think the best of Alex, no matter what.

'Yes, it is,' he said heavily. 'The strongest kind there is.'

They returned to the boarding house to find Bert and Fred pottering about in the kitchen.

Fred was the nightclub bouncer, a vast mountain of a man with a sleepy, contented manner. Little Bert was an amiable ferret.

Gino was instantly at ease with them, chiefly because he wanted to know all about English sport. Soon the three of them were friends for life.

Mrs Baxter returned from school, with Nikki, who gave her mother a brief greeting before claiming her new friend's full attention.

'Let the poor man have a cup of tea before you jump on him,' Laura begged.

'But Mummy I did a picture at school and Gino wants to see it. *Don't you?*'

'Absolutely,' he responded at once. 'I'm longing to see it.'

'Just don't let her be a pest?' Laura said, smiling.

'How can she be a pest?' Gino demanded at once. 'We are friends.'

For half an hour he sat listening, with every sign of interest, as Nikki showed him her picture and explained what it was about. Only when Laura wanted to lay the table did they move.

Sadie and Claudia came in from the factory and Gino immediately asked if there were any jobs available.

'Only in the warehouse, lifting heavy boxes,' Sadie said. 'I expect you want something more exciting.'

'I'll take what I can get,' Gino said. 'I can lift things.'

'In that case, report to the chief packer first thing tomorrow.'

He did so and secured a job that brought him enough to pay his rent and a little to spare. With that he tried to slip back into the life that had been his for the last few months, living from moment to moment.

But he found that refuge was now denied him. Nikki saw to that. She loved nothing better than to talk to him and would pounce, bombarding him with questions.

She was endlessly fascinated by his foreignness, especially his use of Italian words and expressions. The day she first heard *'Assolutamente niente'* she was in seventh heaven.

'It means "absolutely nothing",' she explained to Laura, for perhaps the tenth time.

'Yes, darling, I know what it means.'

'Doesn't it sound lovely? *Assolutamente niente. Assolutamente niente.*'

'If I hear that expression once more,' she seethed to Gino, 'I shall commit murder.'

'Poor Nikki,' he grinned.

'Not her. *You!* This is all your fault.'

At school Nikki boasted of her Italian friend, to such good effect that the geography teacher enquired, via Mrs Baxter, whether Gino would give a talk one afternoon.

'Me?' he demanded hilariously. 'A teacher?'

'You don't have to teach anything,' Nikki hastened to reassure him. 'Just talk about Italy, and how everything's got music and colour, and there are lots of bandits—'

'*Bandits?*'

'Aren't there bandits?' she asked, crestfallen.

'*Assolutamente niente!*' he said firmly, and she giggled.

'Not just one little bandit?' she pleaded.

'Not even half a bandit, you little devil.'

'*Oh, please.*'

It ended, as it was bound to, with him giving his good-natured shrug and agreeing to do what she wanted. He got the afternoon off, and he turned up at the school soon after lunch. He had no idea what he was going to talk about, except that he drew the line at bandits.

Inspiration came when he discovered the pupils were studying Shakespeare's *Romeo and Juliet*. After that he talked about Verona, and the house that purported to be where the Capulets had lived, complete with a real balcony.

The pupils were impressed, especially the older girls who sighed over his good looks. Nikki, who could claim him as a real friend, became the heroine of the hour. It was her proudest moment.

CHAPTER THREE

AFTER that Gino began giving Nikki what he called 'history lessons', but which seemed to concentrate almost entirely on the most bloodthirsty aspects of Italy's past.

'Isn't she a little young to be learning about Lucrezia Borgia?' Laura asked.

'Why? Lucrezia's great fun.'

'I don't suppose her victims thought so. How many is she supposed to have poisoned?'

Gino grinned. 'Between you and me, she probably never poisoned anyone. But don't tell Nikki. She'd be very disappointed.'

Now that he was earning, Gino had increased the rent he paid Laura. She tried to protest, but he said, *'Silenzio!'* with a tone that was unusually imperious for him, and refused to discuss the matter further.

He slipped easily into the life of the boarding house. He was a good listener, always ready to lend a sympathetic ear, and was soon in possession of all the details of the feud between Claudia and Bert. At the best they maintained an armed truce. At the worst they went long periods without speaking. Nikki, who got on famously with both combatants, was adept at taking messages between them.

'Claudia, Bert says did you eat the last cup cake?'

'Bert, Claudia says she was doing you a favour because your waistline—'

'Claudia, Bert says—'

34

And so on. In time, Gino took his own share of messages. He said it made him feel part of the family.

He also set himself to be useful around the house, mending, changing fuses, sometimes cooking the supper.

Three nights a week Laura went out to work, leaving Nikki in the care of the sisters, or Mrs Baxter. Gino would usually spend these evenings doing a little modest carpentry. He'd discovered that Laura tried to economise by buying flat-packed, self-assembly furniture. The plan never worked because she had no gift for putting things together. Since Bert and Fred were equally useless with their hands the house was awash with incomplete items.

Gino went rapidly through three small chests of drawers, to be put in bedrooms, to the infinite gratitude of the occupants, one wardrobe and two bookshelves.

The bookshelves went in the living room where the 'family' congregated to watch television. Nikki was there, going through a photo album, but she looked up to admire.

'You've got the shelves all the same space apart,' she said, awed by this mark of genius.

'It's not that difficult.'

'Well, Mummy can't do it.'

Gino grinned. 'I'd gathered that.'

He got to his feet, brushed himself down and came to look at what she was doing.

'Hey, who's that?' he asked suddenly.

He was pointing at a picture of a young girl in jeans and shirt, with flowing fair hair swirling around her as she did a dance that was clearly energetic. She looked a bit wild, and bit mad, and totally happy.

'Is that who I think it is?' he asked incredulously.

'That was Mummy,' Nikki said, speaking, in the manner of children, as though her mother's earlier self was somebody else, now deceased.

'You mean it *is* Mummy,' Gino suggested.

'No, she doesn't look like that. But she did then. That was before I knew her.'

'Before time began,' Gino said through twitching lips.

He studied the girl again. She was young; heart-breakingly so to anyone who knew how life had treated her later. She'd been perhaps seventeen, and she'd had no idea. She'd just known that life would go exactly as she wanted, the way you always knew that at seventeen.

The next set of pictures came from her dancing career. There she was in leotards, concentrating intensely on the steps she was practising. Then she was dressed up to perform in glittering costumes.

They turned her into almost another person, beautiful, sophisticated, at home in the spotlight. She had *Wow!* legs he noticed with interest, long and elegant as a dancer's should be. Her waist and hips were also *Wow!*

Then there were the wedding pictures. She'd been a joyous bride, gazing at her new husband with radiant eyes as they joined hands on the cake.

He hadn't been looking at her, Gino noted. He was facing the camera with a brilliant grin, as if inviting onlookers to admire his undoubted good looks.

'Full of himself,' Gino thought. Then honesty made him add, 'A bit like I was.'

The recognition didn't make him feel any kinder towards the man. That lovely, fresh, life-enhancing girl deserved better.

The pictures went on. There was Laura, sitting up in

bed, holding baby Nikki, while her husband sat with his arm around both of them, bursting with pride.

'That's my daddy,' Nikki said proudly.

She turned more pages and Gino saw her as a toddler, learning to walk, her hands held by her father. Picture after picture showed them together, and now he could see how she was growing to resemble him. She had his dark hair, his brown eyes, his wide mouth.

One picture showed them looking straight at each other, eyes meeting, sharing smiles of delight as though they recognised their shared looks and rejoiced in them.

After that there was just one more picture, and it said everything. Nikki was about four and now Gino could see the first sign that all was not well. Her forehead had grown, just a little, but an ominous portent of what was to come.

Now it was Laura who sat with her, while her husband kept in the background. His smile had gone, and his face bore a stunned look.

After that he didn't appear in any more pictures.

Gino remembered Laura saying, 'She adored him and he seemed to adore her—then he just upped and left.'

How could any man just switch off his love for a little girl? Unless his 'love' had been little more than vanity?

Gino tried to get into the mind of a man who could simply abandon a child like an unwanted puppy, at the very moment when she needed him most. But he couldn't do it. All he could feel was helpless rage which he concealed behind a smile.

It was the child who turned the pages back to the last picture where the man could be seen.

'That was Daddy,' she said softly, touching the face.

'Yes,' Gino said, floundering for something to say. 'He looks—he looks—quite a fellow.'

'He taught me to swim. He said he'd teach me to draw one day, when I was older. Only he died.'

'Died?' Gino couldn't keep the astonishment out of his voice.

'Yes, he's dead,' Nikki said calmly. 'My daddy's dead.'

Gino drew a long breath, sensing that he was walking across eggshells.

'He'd have been proud of that drawing you showed me,' he said. 'You're very talented.'

She beamed. 'Daddy was good at drawing. I want to be as good as Daddy.'

'I'm sure you will be,' he said lamely. It was the best he could manage while his mind was whirling. Nikki seemed satisfied.

But she had another bombshell for him. As she closed the album she whispered, 'Don't tell Mum what we talked about. She doesn't know that I know, and I don't want to worry her.'

He nodded, bereft of speech. He was aghast.

When Nikki had gone to bed he took a walk through the quiet streets. The last of the summer night was fading, and by the time he was ready to turn back it was completely dark.

Just ahead of him was a pub, with a sign proclaiming The Running Sheep, and he felt in need of a beer after this evening. Inside, it was a small, attractive place with a pleasant, old-fashioned atmosphere. The barman sold him a pint of bitter, and he went to sit at a table in the corner.

He was tired. What he'd heard tonight had disturbed him, but his walk had left him no clearer how to deal with it. It was pleasant to sit there, sipping and thinking about nothing very much.

He closed his eyes, and might have dozed off for a moment. When he opened them the barman had gone. In his place was a young woman with fair curly hair and a sweet smile. It took Gino a moment to realise that he was looking at Laura.

He was so used to regarding her as a landlady and Nikki's mother that he'd unconsciously been perceiving her through those filters, and they had gotten in the way of the real woman. Now he realised that the dancer he had seen in the photographs was still alive somewhere. It was like seeing her for the first time.

She was talking to a customer, almost seeming to flirt with him, shaking her head so that the curls danced about her face. It was a young face, much younger than Gino had realised, and charming, especially when she smiled.

It had a lot in common with the girl in the pictures, except that her blazing belief in life had gone for ever. This woman was more cautious, hurt and vulnerable, but also more interesting than before.

The customer was elderly, and clearly delighted by the attention. He paid for his drink and would have lingered if the barman hadn't returned, looking at his watch.

'Last orders, ladies and gentlemen,' he announced.

The company was thin tonight, and she was soon finished. Gino waved to catch her attention, and they slipped out into the street together.

'So this is where you sneak away in the evenings,' he said, grinning. 'No wonder you don't want to be at home when you can be surrounded by suitors here.'

'Oh, stop that. Sam's a dear old boy and nobody's

flirted with him for years. It's part of the job, and mostly innocent.'

'Mostly?' he asked, glancing sideways.

'Nothing I can't handle. I've got a mean left hook. Want me to demonstrate?'

'I'll take your word for it,' he said hastily. 'Let's go home.'

It was pleasant walking home under the stars, and Gino was reluctant to spoil their peace, but he had no choice.

'There's something you need to know,' he said heavily. 'Nikki told me tonight that her father is dead.'

Laura stopped and faced him, horrified.

'She said what?'

'She was showing me some family pictures, and when he disappeared from them she said, "My daddy's dead".'

'Oh, no,' she breathed. 'He didn't die. He walked out.'

'Do you ever hear from him?'

'Not since the divorce. He doesn't stay in touch.'

'Christmas? Birthdays?'

'Not a word, not a card. I suppose it's easier for her to think of him as dead than neglectful.'

'Any chance she actually believes it?'

'No, if he was dead, I'd have told her. She must know that.'

'So it's her way of comforting herself.' Gino sighed. 'I'm not supposed to have told you this. She said you didn't know that she knew, and she didn't want to worry you.'

'Oh, God, she's so sweet and generous.'

'Yes, she is, but I've betrayed her confidence. I had to. I couldn't have kept a thing like that to myself—'

'Of course you did the right thing. But I've been so stupid. Why didn't I see it coming? How could I have left her exposed to this?'

'Hey, hey, don't blame yourself,' he said urgently. '*You* didn't expose her to this. *He* did.'

'But I should have thought. Oh, heavens!'

Her voice was husky with tears and she buried her face in her hands. Gino put his arms about her, holding her tightly while she wept.

'It isn't your fault,' he said again. 'You're her mother, but you can only do so much. There are things you can't make right for her, however hard you try. You can see them coming, but you can't get out of the way.'

'But I could help her through them. I've got to get home quickly, and talk to her.'

'No, don't.' In his agitation he took her arms and drew her around to face him. 'Stop and think. What are you going to tell her, that I betrayed her confidence?'

'Confidence? She's an eight-year-old child—'

'Even a child likes to be treated with respect. Right now, she feels she can talk to me.'

'But why not me?'

'Because you're her mother. I'm not involved so it's easier for her to talk to me. As long as she trusts me, maybe I can be of some use to her, and to you. Laura please, don't do anything to make her stop trusting me.'

He felt some of the tension go out of her, and she sighed, nodding.

'You're right,' she said in despair. 'I should have thought of that.'

'You've got to stop blaming yourself for everything. You keep saying you should have done this and you should have done that, but you can't do it all. No one can. Let someone else share the load.'

She gave a wry laugh.

'There's never been anyone to share it with.'

'You've got me now,' he reminded her gently.

She gave a shaky laugh. 'Yes, I have, haven't I?' She put her arms about him and kissed him on the cheek. 'How did I ever manage before you arrived? The best kid brother I never had.'

'What do you mean, *kid*?'

'I'm three years older than you. That makes you my kid brother. And, like most kid brothers, you can sometimes be a pain in the butt, and at other times be pretty marvellous.'

'Yes, I finished the shelves,' he said at once.

'I didn't mean—oh, *you!*'

He hugged her. 'Come on, let's go home. Your baby brother is starving.'

He made spaghetti and tomato sauce, which they ate together at the kitchen table.

Laura got out the photo album and he went through it again.

'You were a real looker, weren't you?' he observed.

'Yes, I was—the dim and distant past.'

'That's not what I—'

'Oh, shut up!' She thumped him amiably and he just managed not to drop tomato sauce on the album.

'You can tell so much from old photos,' he mused. 'People's past selves, sometimes even they've forgotten what they were like—and there they are.'

'What about you? Don't you have any record of your past self?'

She felt him tense.

'Not here with me.'

'Not one little picture of the younger Gino?'

After a moment he said quietly, 'All right.'

He went up to his room and returned a moment later with a picture that he put into her hand.

It showed Gino, with flowers in his disarranged hair, looking mildly tipsy, his arm about the loveliest young woman Laura had ever seen. She was blonde and elegant, with the kind of supreme assurance that roused Laura's envy. She and Gino were laughing at each other against a background of coloured lights and revelry.

Laura studied her, wondering if this was the answer to Gino's habit of seeming to live life at arm's length. He was always good-natured and kind, but she knew now that he kept the world at a distance, never quite involving himself in the moment.

'I've never seen you look like that,' she said, her eyes on the brilliant young face. 'Not just happy, but throwing yourself into everything and hang the consequences. You learned caution after this.'

He nodded.

'Was it very long ago?' she asked.

'Last year. A thousand years. Another universe.'

She sighed. 'I know what you mean. You never know what's waiting for you just around the corner, do you?'

'I guess not.'

'Thank you for showing me.' She handed him back the picture and he took it without a word.

After that they went on talking about nothing much until it was time to go to bed. It was cosy, unexciting, the kind of evening Gino would once have despised. But, bit by bit, he found he was losing the appetite for anything livelier. He could not have said why.

The next evening Laura had another stint in The Running Sheep.

The first hour was busy and she was run off her feet,

but at last the crowd thinned out and she was able to turn her attention to a man who had been waiting patiently at the far end of the bar.

'I'm so sorry,' she said.

'Don't worry, I can see how it is.' He gave her a pleasant grin.

He was about forty, with a reassuring solidity, but he was also handsome in a slightly cinematic way. His hair was thick and fair, his eyes deep blue, his features regular, only just beginning to blur.

She served him a whisky and he took it with the same charming grin, raising the glass in salute.

'Have one with me,' he said.

'Thanks, I'll have an orange juice.'

After that, if she had a free moment she returned to him. His name was Steve Deyton, and he was making frequent visits to the neighbourhood, with a view to setting up a factory making stationery products.

'I don't know anyone in this area,' he said, 'and there's very little to do in the evenings. I've been here several times, hoping you'd notice me, but you never did.'

She laughed. It was a familiar gambit, and one to which she had a standard repertoire of answers. In fact she had noticed him, but she wasn't prepared to say so. Not yet. She gave him a light-hearted reply, and went away to serve someone else.

At the end of the evening he asked if he could give her a lift home.

'Thank you, that would be—' Laura stopped, her attention caught by something she saw in the corner. 'No, I don't think so. Thank you anyway.'

He followed her gaze. 'I see. A boyfriend?'

'No,' she laughed. 'My brother. Goodnight.'

Laura put on her coat and headed for the corner.

'Hey,' she said, shaking Gino's shoulder. 'Wake up.'

'Hm? Oh, hello.'

'It's time to go.'

He looked at the half full glass of beer.

'It's flat,' he mourned. 'How long since I dozed off?'

'I don't know. I didn't know you were here.'

'No, your boss served me. All right, I'm coming.'

He hauled himself sleepily out of his seat and followed her out into the street, dropping a casual hand on her shoulder.

'You may have to support me home,' he said.

'How many did you have before you fell asleep?'

'No idea. That's the idea of falling asleep. It wipes the slate clean.'

'Does it?' she asked severely.

'Oh, hush, you sound like a grandmother.'

'You make me feel like a grandmother,' she said. 'Or an aunt. You need looking after.'

'Wash your hands of me,' he said gloomily. 'I'm a hopeless case.'

She said no more until they were in the kitchen.

'Sit,' she said, pointing to a chair.

'Like I'm a dog,' he protested.

'Yes. Now be a good boy and *sit*.'

He did so, and remained there obediently while she put on the kettle, and went upstairs to check on Nikki. When she returned the kettle was boiling and she made instant coffee, which she set before him.

That brought him to life.

'*English coffee*? Instant? Good grief woman, are you trying to kill me?'

'No, I'm trying to sober you up.'

He gave her a look and, rising, started to make real

coffee in the percolator, both of which he had bought and presented to the kitchen. Laura smiled quietly to herself. At least she'd got him going.

The coffee he set before her was perfect, strong, sweet-smelling, *Italian.*

'Mm,' she said appreciatively.

'You must let me teach you to make coffee,' he growled.

'Nah, it's wasted on the English.'

'True.'

They sat in companionable silence for a while.

'So, who is she?' Laura risked asking at last.

'Who's who?'

'The woman in the photo last night. That is what this is all about, isn't it?'

For a moment she thought he would slide away from the question, but at last he said, 'Her name is Alex. She came to Tuscany last year. She'd inherited a claim on our farm.'

'Our?'

'My brother, Rinaldo, and me.' Gino's voice became wry and slightly cynical. 'We couldn't afford to pay her, so it was obvious one of us would have to marry her. We tossed a coin.'

'You *what*?'

'We tossed a coin. Don't say it—' he held up a hand as if to ward her off. 'Disgraceful, despicable, chauvinist, anything you like. And I'll tell you something that'll annoy you even more. Rinaldo won, and immediately said he wasn't interested and she was all mine.' He grinned. 'If you could see your face!'

'The pair of you deserve to have your heads banged together. I hope she taught you both a lesson.'

He was silent a moment before saying quietly, 'Let's just say that she made her own choice.'

'And it wasn't you?' she said gently.

He shrugged.

Her brief indignation died. Whatever boyish games he'd played at the start, the result had devastated him, so that now he was still wandering in a wilderness.

'You seemed to be having fun in that picture,' she said.

'That was the Feast of St Romauld, last year, in Florence. The three of us went together. I don't even remember when the picture was taken, but it was a good evening.'

Suddenly he said, 'It's dangerous to laugh.'

'Why?' she asked.

'People think that's all you can do. "Oh, it's only Gino. He'll laugh it off. All life is a joke to him." Only then—suddenly it isn't funny—but they don't realise. And you can start hating people.'

'I can't imagine you hating anyone,' Laura said.

'It's frighteningly easy when you get started. You have to keep reminding yourself that these are people you mustn't hate, because if you do, you've got no one left to love. But then—'

His voice trailed off into silence. He was looking at something she couldn't see. Laura wondered if he still knew that she was there.

'Gino,' she said softly, laying a hand on his arm.

He made a sudden sound of impatience. 'Listen to me. I'm getting maudlin.'

'I'm a good listener,' she said.

'Thanks but there's nothing to talk about. Love comes and goes every day.'

'Not real love. If it's very real and true—as I think

it was with you—it changes the course of your life. It changes *you*. Gino, I'm not trying to pry, truly, but you're always there if I need a shoulder to cry on. Can't I do the same for you?'

He smiled. 'Bless you, but who's crying? I got over Alex months ago.'

And if you believed that, Laura thought, you'd believe anything. But it was clear that he'd confided more than he'd meant to, and was now backtracking in self-protection.

He squeezed her hand briefly and went upstairs to bed.

CHAPTER FOUR

THE man at the bar was the same one who'd claimed Laura's attention the night before. Gino recalled seeing him just before he himself had nodded off.

He seemed to be in his early forties, tall, heavily built, with a good head of hair, expensively dressed. When he laughed he showed white, regular teeth. Surveying him critically, Gino supposed that many women would have called him handsome. Certainly Laura seemed to enjoy his company. She was laughing freely and with no sign of tension.

For a moment she was the girl of the snapshots, before grief and worry wore her down. Some part of that girl was still there, he thought, just as her face was still beautiful with that light glowing from within.

The man seized her hand and kissed the back of it. She remonstrated, but not very severely. It took a wave from another customer to recall her to her duties, looking flushed and a little embarrassed.

Gino slipped quietly out of the pub.

At home he lay on his bed, fully dressed, and went downstairs when he heard Laura come in. She was in the kitchen, humming as she made the tea. She pointed to a cup and he nodded.

'You sound happy,' he said.

'No, not especially,' she said with a touch of self-consciousness. 'Well, maybe a bit.'

'A good evening in the pub?'

'Yes, business was brisk.'

'I expect you meet a lot of smart-asses, who think a barmaid is fair game,' he said casually.

'You know I do. You've seen them.'

'I don't mean the old boys, but the younger ones might be more of a handful.'

'I know how to deal with them. Nobody fools with me.'

'Nobody?'

'Not unless I let them.'

'Oh,' he said. 'Oh.'

'Is something the matter?'

'Nothing,' he said hastily.

'You sounded funny.'

'I'm just a bit tired. I'll drink this and go to bed.'

He was a little put out by her refusal to confide in him. They were supposed to be friends, weren't they?

But he told himself that it was her business if she didn't want to talk about it. And with that he had to be satisfied.

Every morning, in the packing department, a variety of attractive young women would compete to bring Gino his tea.

'He's got all the girls sighing for him,' Claudia said at the boarding house one night. 'You should see Maisie and Jill, practically scratching each other's eyes out for one of his smiles.'

'That's not Maisie and Jill,' Gino said, playing up to her. 'It's Lily and Rose, or do I mean Patsy and Cindy, or—'

'All right, big-head,' Claudia quenched him.

'I take it you're enjoying your job,' Laura teased.

'It has its moments,' he admitted.

'Are they all your girlfriends?' Nikki demanded with innocent fascination.

'All of them,' Gino confirmed solemnly.

'Have you got lots and lots of girlfriends?'

'Lots and lots and *lots*,' he said.

'Why you and not the others?' she wanted to know.

'Because I'm Italian, and Italy is the land of Casanova.'

'Who was Casanova?'

Gino opened his mouth and closed it again.

'Serve you right,' Laura said, laughing. 'When will you learn to be careful what you say to Nikki?'

'Why has he got to be careful, Mummy?'

'Eat your tea,' she said hastily.

Mercifully Nikki allowed the subject to drop, and it wasn't raised again until she'd gone to bed, and Sadie declared with relish, 'They're taking bets all over the factory. The hot money's on Tess.'

'Which one is Tess?' Claudia wanted to know.

'You know, the little sexpot with red hair, always sashaying around the place putting all the goods on display.' Sadie made an exaggerated figure eight with her hands. 'They say she's a proper little raver. Isn't that right, Gino?'

But Gino was on his guard by now, and although he winked knowingly, all he said was, 'Ladies, my lips are sealed.'

They would have been astonished to learn the truth. In fact, they would not have believed it. Tess had a voluptuous figure and big blue eyes, but behind those eyes was a steely efficiency, as Gino had discovered on the day she explained exactly what she wanted of him.

'I'm gonna kill that rat, Perry,' she'd muttered, handing Gino his tea one morning.

'I thought you were crazy about him.'

'I am, but I'm gonna kill him. His roving eye has roved too far this time. Quick, he's coming. Smile at me.'

Slipping into his allotted role, Gino gave her an infatuated smile right under Perry's nose. Thereafter they played out the farce whenever necessary and so far it had kept Perry almost, if not entirely, faithful.

They would leave work together, or meet for a drink in the evening. There was a decent pub near work, but it was an ugly, beery place, a dump.

'Let's go to The Running Sheep,' Gino suggested. 'That'll teach Perry you're worth something better than this place.'

Heads turned in their direction as they entered. Tess's blatant charms made a stunning impact, and Gino had a feeling as if the old days had returned. He'd been the man who could get any girl, who played the field as if life contained nothing better. Which had been true, once.

He saw Tess seated and approached Laura at the bar.

'A bottle of champagne, please.'

She glanced at his companion. 'Let me guess. It's Maisie—or Jill, or Rose, or Lily—'

'Cut it out,' he said, grinning. 'That's Tess.'

'The sexpot! Wow! Yes, I can see that you've got something to celebrate.'

He ground his teeth. 'Will you just get me some champagne, please?'

'Yes, *sir*!'

'To think I used to wish I had a sister! I didn't know how lucky I was.'

She handed him the bottle and two champagne glasses. 'Not all women are as bossy as me.'

'Now there's something to be thankful for. How much?'

She told him.

'Don't you have anything cheaper?' he asked plaintively.

'You skinflint. I've a good mind to warn her what you're really like.'

'She wouldn't believe you,' he assured her. 'Nobody would.'

'Oh, get out of here.'

Laughing, he offered her the money, then realised that he'd lost her attention. 'Laura?'

She quickly looked away from the door, back to him. 'Sorry. Oh yes, the money.'

Even as she took it her eyes were fixed on someone passing behind him.

'Hi, Steve,' she said, smiling. 'Be with you in a minute.'

'I can wait if it's for you,' he replied.

It was him, taking his seat at the bar and waiting for Laura with an easy assurance that Gino found obscurely offensive.

Tess eyed the champagne with glee. 'If Perry could only see me now! He asked me out tonight. I said no thanks, I had other plans. He said, "What other plans?" and I said, "Never you mind." I wonder if that was the right way to play it. What do you think, Gino? *Gino?*'

'Sorry,' he said hastily.

'Why are you staring at the barmaid?'

'I was wondering if she gave me the right change. Never mind. You were saying about Perry.'

'Did I do the right thing?'

'Absolutely.'

He had no idea what she was talking about. The man

Laura had called Steve was accepting his drink, indicating for her to have one too. They looked like people who knew each other well.

'I want to make him jealous,' Tess mused, 'but not so jealous that I'll lose him.'

'It's a difficult decision,' Gino agreed mechanically.

They were laughing, heads together over the bar. Gino forced himself to look away.

'Do you really want to keep him?' he asked Tess for something to say. 'If he isn't faithful now, he isn't going to improve.'

'Well, all men fool around, don't they?' she said gloomily. 'That bloke at the bar is trying to fool around with the barmaid.'

'Is that what he's trying to do?' Gino murmured.

'Yes, just watch him gazing into her eyes—'

'I am.'

'He's probably got a wife somewhere.'

'Well, it's their business,' Gino said in a voice that was slightly tense. 'I'm sure she can take care of herself. Let's not watch them.'

As she had promised Gino, Laura hadn't spoken to Nikki about her father, and the child's insistence that he was dead. Nor had Nikki mentioned it again, and the subject seemed to be safely over.

They were coming up to the little girl's ninth birthday.

'It's a big milestone,' Gino told her gravely.

'No, ten is a big milestone,' she said, 'because it's double figures.'

'But nine is the last one before that,' Gino explained. 'You'll be in double figures the rest of your life—unless you live to be a hundred, when you'll go into triple figures.'

Nikki giggled.

'So, this is your last year in single figures, and we must mark the occasion properly.'

Satisfied with this explanation Nikki went off to tell Bert and Fred all about it. Laura shook her head and said admiringly, 'How do you always manage to say the right thing to her?'

He gave a comical shrug. 'My brother Rinaldo would say it came from having the mind of a child myself. He's probably right.'

His own gift to Nikki was a lavishly illustrated book about Italy, with text in both Italian and English.

'She'll love this,' Laura said, looking through it with delight. They were talking late at night, as they often did.

'What are you giving her?'

'A new dress, and some shoes I know she wants. And look at this.'

Laura darted into the next room and returned with a bag from which she took a book about horses, and a birthday card.

'I'm going to give her this,' she said, 'from Jack.'

'*What?*'

'I'll sign it "from Daddy". Then she'll feel that he still remembers her, and she'll be able to let go of this fantasy about him being dead.'

Gino clutched his head. 'No, Laura, please no, you mustn't do this.'

'But it's what she needs.'

'It's the last thing she needs,' he said, horrified. 'She won't believe it, and that will make things worse.'

'Of course she'll believe it. Why shouldn't she?'

'Because she's very bright and not easily fooled. And even if she does believe it, think what'll happen. She'll ask you a lot of questions that you won't know how to answer. It's a mad idea.'

'Gino, please, I'm only trying to give her a little happiness. I'm just so glad you told me the way her mind was working.'

'I'm beginning to wish I hadn't.' In his urgency Gino took hold of her shoulders. 'Laura, listen to me. Nikki isn't just intelligent, she's strong and brave, and she's worked out a way of coping.'

'Coping? Telling herself stories—'

'She's invented that fantasy because she needs it. It keeps her going. When she doesn't need it any more she'll abandon it, but she has to pick the moment. Don't try to force her.'

Suddenly she was angry.

'Gino, I know what I'm doing. She's my daughter, and I think I know what's best for her.'

He made a wry grimace and dropped his hands, turning away as he did so. At once Laura was horrified at herself.

'Oh, no, I'm sorry! I didn't mean that. You've been so good to both of us—'

'Well, I suppose you're right,' he sighed. 'She's your child and you know her better than I do. I'm sorry, Laura. Please forget I said anything.'

'If only I knew what was the right thing to do! I never do know, you see. It's always a choice of two wrongs.'

'I know,' he said gently. 'And I just worry and confuse you. You're her mother, and I have no right to interfere.'

When the day came, everyone in the boarding house brought Nikki gifts and cards, and left them stacked by her place at breakfast. It was a Saturday so she didn't have to rush.

'All for me?' she asked, eyes shining.

'Every single one, my darling,' Laura told her.

One by one the child opened her cards and gifts, exclaiming with delight over everything.

Finally there was one left. Laura had kept it back on purpose. Nikki opened the card, a big, lavish one with the words, 'Happy Birthday to my daughter' emblazoned in gilt letters.

She frowned, reading the verse, looking at where it read, *Thinking of you, darling, with love, Daddy.*

'Why, it's from Daddy,' Laura said brightly. 'Isn't that nice?'

But Nikki dropped the card as though it had stung her. 'It's not from Daddy,' she said in a deadly quiet voice.

'Darling, it is—'

'It's not from Daddy—' Her words were coming jerkily now. 'It's not from Daddy because—because Daddy's dead—he's dead—he's dead—'

'Darling—' Laura touched her gently. 'Daddy isn't dead—'

'He is, he is,' Nikki cried. 'That's why he never comes to see me, because he's dead, *he's dead.*'

She burst out crying bitterly, burying her face in her arms on the table. Her shoulders heaved with sobs.

Gino closed his eyes.

The others slipped quietly away, knowing that they had no place here. Laura put her arms around Nikki and drew her child close. Her face was distraught as she realised the catastrophic mistake she had made.

'Darling,' she said soothingly, 'darling, oh, my darling—I'm so sorry.'

Gino began to move to the door, but over Nikki's shoulder Laura's eyes frantically met his. With a little shake of her head she begged him not to go.

He hesitated. Much as he longed to help, this was surely something that Nikki and her mother must resolve together. He was afraid of making things worse. But he couldn't ignore the appeal in Laura's eyes, or the heartbroken sobs coming from the child.

'Nikki,' Laura was saying, stroking her head, 'let me—'

But she was checked by a shriek. Nikki flung her mother's hand off and jumped up from the chair.

'Daddy's dead!' she screamed. 'He's dead, he's dead, he's dead! I hate you, I hate you.'

Tears were pouring down Laura's face.

'Daddy loved me,' Nikki screamed, 'and if—if he was alive he'd be here, and he'd give me a present and a card. He wouldn't go away and leave me because he loved me best in all the world. You're a liar *and I hate you.*'

Her voice rose to a shriek of anguish. Wail after wail poured from her while her arms flailed in all directions, as if she would fend off the whole world. When Laura tried to reach for her Nikki lashed out, refusing to allow her mother near her.

'Nikki, please,' Laura begged.

The little girl's only answer was another shriek. The misery of years, bottled up, had finally been released in an unstoppable explosion.

Appalled by such agony, Gino realised that neither words nor reason would be any help now. Only one thing could help, and he did it.

Dropping to his knees in front of Nikki he put his arms around her and drew her tightly against him, ignoring her flailing fists that pummelled madly against his head and shoulders.

At last Nikki gave up fighting him and stood with her arms about his neck, sobbing violently.

'*Povera piccina,*' he murmured. '*Povera piccina.*'

She went on crying, and he let her do so, not trying to calm her, except by the firm pressure of his arms, with their silent message of safety and affection. He knew she must end this in her own good time.

Laura watched them, devastated, yet desperately thankful that there was someone for the two of them to cling onto.

It seemed to take a long time, but at last Nikki's tears abated. Too exhausted to weep any more, she just stood, clinging to Gino, hiccuping.

'*Piccina,*' he said softly.

'Yes?'

'You're strangling me.'

Nikki gave a choking laugh and slightly loosened her grip. But she did not release him. He was safety.

'Your poor Momma,' he chided gently. 'You frightened her.'

'Sorry,' Nikki whispered.

'It's all right, darling,' Laura said.

There was an ominous pause. They were in a minefield.

'We'll talk about it later,' Gino said firmly. 'Much later. Now we have important things to do.'

'What important things?' Nikki asked huskily.

'We have a funfair to go to. There's one in the park. I think they put it there to celebrate your birthday.'

Disengaging herself from Gino's arms Nikki hugged her mother.

'I didn't mean it, Mummy. I just—I just—'

'It's all right,' Laura said quickly. 'It's really all right. Why don't you go and wash your face?'

She was talking for the sake of talking, anything to let the dangerous moment slip past. When Nikki had gone away she said desperately, 'Are we going to let it hang in the air, with nothing settled?'

'It might be best,' Gino said. 'She's told you what she needs to believe. You can't confirm it, but you don't have to deny it. Just let it go for a while.'

'I should have listened to you,' Laura admitted. 'But I thought she'd like to hear from him.'

'She prefers to think of him as dead,' Gino said sadly, 'because death is easier to cope with than rejection. A present and a card are all very well, but he wasn't here, was he? She knows they weren't really from him, just as, in her heart, she knows he's abandoned her. But she doesn't *want* to know it yet. She wants to go on believing in him, and you threatened that.'

She gazed at him, shaking her head in wonder. 'How do you understand so much?'

He'd been puzzling about that himself, mystified at his own instinctive knowledge. But now the conscious memory came back to him.

'I once consoled myself with a similar fantasy,' he said in a tone of discovery. 'My mother died when I was about Nikki's age, and for a long time I wouldn't let myself believe it. I'm nearly ten years younger than my brother, so I suppose she made a favourite of me, the way the baby of the family tends to become a favourite.

'I just couldn't face the fact that she'd gone away for ever. So I told myself she was still alive. I used to talk to my father about her, as though she was coming home at any moment.

'And Poppa always played up to me. For my sake he'd talk as though she was coming home at any moment, although it must have broken his heart. He was a very wise and loving man.'

Gino stopped and seemed lost in a reverie. Laura had a feeling that their surroundings had vanished and he could see again the Tuscan farmhouse where he'd spent his happy childhood.

'What happened?' she asked after a while.

'On the first anniversary of her death I saw Poppa and Rinaldo getting ready to go out, dressed in their Sunday best. I knew, without anything being said, that they were going to visit her grave. Poppa looked at me, with a question in his eyes, and I put my best clothes on and went with them. I could cope with it then, you see, because Poppa let me pick my own moment.

'It's harder for Nikki than it was for me. As I said, death can be endured. It's rejection that's unbearable.'

'And I can't help her there, can I?' Laura brooded. She took Gino's hand. 'But you can. Only you, it seems, because you're a man and she can imagine you in her father's place.'

'You know I'll do anything she needs. I can stay with her today if you like. Later on we'll go to the funfair, the three of us, and anyone else who wants to come.'

In the event the entire household went. Since it was the early evening Bert and Fred weren't due to go to work until later.

Gino found a stall selling huge silly hats with broad brims, and bought some for himself, Laura and Nikki. Nikki's covered most of her forehead, leaving her nothing to worry about but enjoying herself.

Everyone halted at the huge roller coaster. Only Nikki was really eager to go on it. Bert and Fred didn't even pretend not to be cowards. Laura gulped and said she thought she could manage, but Nikki took firm hold of Gino's hand and said, 'Come on.'

'I'm not scared,' he told Laura faintly. 'I'm not scared, I'm not scared, I'm not—*all right, Nikki, don't pull!*'

At the top of the first long drop there was a camera, clicking away at everyone as they reached the last moment before the ghastly descent. Once back on the ground they bought the picture. It showed Nikki full of exhilaration while Gino regarded the drop with stark, wide-eyed horror. They all had a lot of fun with that.

Later that night, when everyone else was in bed, Gino said awkwardly, 'Laura, you mustn't mind that Nikki clings to me a little. You're her mother, and I'm a stranger—'

'You're not a stranger,' Laura said quickly. 'You never could be. I'm not jealous. I'm grateful to whichever fate sent you to us.'

Suddenly she made a swift movement, taking his head between her hands and kissing him briefly on the lips.

'That's for being wonderful,' she said, and went away before he could say anything.

Whichever fate sent you. The words resounded in his head. More and more he'd felt that he had no control over what happened to him, that he was merely following signposts.

Gino would have been the first to admit that he'd been irresponsible most of his life, having little reason to be otherwise. The events that had driven him from his home had matured him, but also shipwrecked him.

Then a little girl, in dreadful need, had taken his hand and said, 'You, and nobody else.'

There was no escape.

But he didn't feel wonderful. When he thought of failing her he felt terrified.

CHAPTER FIVE

A FEW evenings later Gino came in from work to find Nikki eagerly poring over a mail-order catalogue, selling clothes.

'That one,' she said decisively, pointing to a blue dress that seemed to be made of some floaty material, perhaps chiffon.

'It's a little old for you,' Gino said, considering it.

'Not me, Mummy. She's got a date.'

'A date? Who with?'

Nikki giggled. 'Didn't you know she's got a boyfriend?'

'Yes, I did,' he said gruffly. 'I've seen him.'

'What's he like?'

'Fat and old.'

'He is not,' Laura said, coming in from the kitchen. 'He's in his forties. That's not old.'

'He's fat.'

'He's strongly built. Gino stop this. I don't know why you've taken "agin" Steve. He's a nice man.'

'Nice is as nice does,' Gino growled.

'And what does that mean?'

It didn't mean anything and he knew it. He couldn't have explained why the thought of Laura on a date with Steve disturbed him, but as a good brother he was going to object.

Not in front of Nikki, however. For her sake he decided to fade into the background while Laura studied Nikki's choice of dress.

'It's a bit young for me,' she demurred.

'But you *are* young, Mummy.'

'Thank you darling, but I'm thirty-two. That's quite old.'

'It's too young for a man of forty-five,' Gino growled.

'That's for me to say,' Laura said, edgily. 'Will you please keep your nose out of my business?'

Gino didn't reply, but he looked so crestfallen that Nikki said, 'Poor Gino! Mummy's rotten to you.'

'She is, isn't she?' he said, sounding hurt.

'But why?'

'I don't know.' He sighed forlornly.

She put her arms about him. 'You've got me,' she comforted him.

'*Grazie, piccina.* Now I don't mind so much.'

'You're hopeless, the pair of you!' Laura said in exasperation. 'Gino, stop acting the fool!'

'But I *am* a fool,' he defended himself. 'You've always known that.' To Nikki he confided, 'She's being rotten to me again.'

They solemnly nodded together.

Laura gave a choke of laughter, and her brief annoyance died. She didn't know why Gino was suddenly in an awkward mood, but he'd more than redeemed himself.

'All right,' she said, 'I'm sorry I was rotten. Now let me see that dress again, darling. How much is it? Hm!'

Sadie and Claudia came in and exclaimed over the dress and its suitability for Laura. Mrs Baxter, arriving later, was also pleased, adding, 'And you should splash out on a really good hairdresser.'

Gino went up to his room, wondering if he was the

only person in the house who hadn't taken leave of his senses.

It got worse. Bert and Fred, on their way out to work, were united in the opinion that blue was Laura's colour and she should go for it.

When the meal was over Gino helped Laura with the washing-up.

'What are you playing at?' he demanded. 'That fellow's a slime ball.'

'How would you know?' she demanded, indignant that he wouldn't let it drop.

'I've seen him kissing your hand,' was the best he could manage.

'Oh, really! Have you never kissed a woman's hand?'

'Of course I have, but that's different. I'm Italian. It's expected.'

'Who expects it?'

'The tourists. The girls arrive looking for romance. It's part of the holiday, so you kiss their hands, you tell them they're beautiful, and then you—that is, they— *why am I telling you all this?*'

'Because you forgot to be cautious,' she said, scoring a disconcerting bull's-eye. 'So that's where you honed your English?'

'Yes, it was almost always English girls,' he admitted. 'The others don't fall for it so easily.'

She regarded him satirically.

'In any case,' he added, suddenly awkward, 'I'm not like that any more, I only meant—'

'That's it's all right for you to kiss women's hands, but if Steve does it, he's a slime ball.'

'*I* was a slime ball. We all were, me and Franco and Carlo and Mario and Enrico and—'

'All right, I get the picture.'

'If you want the ugly truth, when the tourist season arrived we used to count the girls getting off the planes.'

'You're a real charmer, you know that?'

'I was. It was my stock-in-trade. But not now. I grew out of it.' He added significantly, 'Some men never grow out of it.'

'So you judge him on the basis of one moment, observed from a distance. Well, if that's the worst you can say about him I don't think I'll worry.' A sudden devilish imp made her add crossly, 'And if we're talking about characters out of a bad film, how about your lady friend? All teeth 'n' tits!'

The robust expression, coming from her, made him stare. *'What?'* he demanded, half shocked, half laughing.

'You know who I mean. Vulgarity personified. Don't you lecture me about who I go out with.'

Since he could hardly admit that Tess was using him Gino backed off. 'I am not—I'm merely trying to stop you making a mistake.' He recalled something Tess had said. 'He's probably got a wife somewhere.'

'He hasn't. He's a widower.'

'He says.'

Then Laura lost her temper. Closing the kitchen door so that nobody could hear her she turned on Gino, eyes blazing.

'I'm going out with a man for Pete's sake! I am over the age of twenty-one. I make my own decisions. Do you know the last time I had a night out? A nice man is taking me out to dinner, and then we may go dancing. And you have nothing to say about it.'

Confronted by her glittering eyes and the hair falling in wispy curls over her forehead, Gino held up his hands and backed off.

'Fine,' he said. 'Fine. I'll get out of your way.'

He eased himself quietly out of the door. Left alone, Laura picked up a tea towel and hurled it angrily into a corner.

She ordered the dress by telephone next morning and it arrived two days later. The whole family demanded to see it, and she paraded up and down for them, turning this way and that like a model.

'Oh Mummy, you do look pretty!' Nikki sighed.

There was a murmur of confirmation, and Mrs Baxter said, 'Now you book that hairdressing appointment without delay.'

Gino alone said nothing.

The date with Steve was set for three days ahead. In the afternoon she drove into town to the hairdresser. But when she returned it was raining cats and dogs, and she sat in the car, staring out helplessly.

The whole boarding-house family, watching from the window, saw her predicament.

'Right, this calls for clever tactics,' Gino said. 'I'll go out with the umbrella, Nikki, you stand at the door and make sure it's wide open.'

Nikki nodded like a trusty lieutenant, and took up position at the front door, while Gino snatched the big umbrella from the hall stand and darted down the steps, fighting to open it, and getting soaked.

At the car door a little dance took place as he fought to keep the umbrella over her head as she emerged, lock the car door, then shepherd her up the stairs and through the door.

At last the operation was complete and they could all congratulate themselves.

'You look fantastic!' Nikki declared breathlessly.

Gino, rubbing his sodden hair with his handkerchief,

grunted. She did look fantastic. She looked the way she ought to look, the way she would look all the time if she didn't have to spend her whole life working and worrying.

Now she had the chance of a break and he'd tried to spoil it for her.

'You look lovely,' he said, emerging from the handkerchief.

She turned. 'Do I really?' she asked, beaming at him but half pleading too, as though his opinion mattered most.

'Wonderful,' he said quietly. *'Bellissima.'*

'I'll just get supper, and then I can put on the dress.'

'You can't cook supper,' he said, appalled. 'The heat will send your hair floppy. Stay out of the kitchen. I'll do it. *Does anybody mind pasta?'*

Gino's pasta had become an institution, and for the next hour the kitchen was cheerfully chaotic. Laura came downstairs just as they finished eating, and silence fell.

Now she had not only the hairstyle, but make-up and the dress, which came into its own with the proper extras. Her eyes seemed a deeper blue, and there was a gleam of excitement in them.

'How do I look?' she asked, twirling.

'He won't have anything to complain of,' Gino observed.

There was a general outcry against this moderate praise, but he ignored it, taking his jacket from a hook and saying, 'Your carriage awaits, Cinderella.'

'How do you mean?'

'You said he was collecting you at the pub, so I'll drive you there. Luckily it's stopped raining.'

There was no sign of Steve when they reached The

Running Sheep. Laura left the car and stood on the corner, and Gino got out to wait with her.

'Prince Charming is supposed to be on time,' he observed.

'Don't start. He probably got held up in traffic.'

'I'm just pointing out that on a first date it's usual to pay the lady the compliment of being punctual.'

'I don't know why you're so tetchy.'

'I'm not tetchy,' he said too quickly.

'Yes, you are, you've been tetchy for days. It's not like you.'

'You don't know what's like me. Actually I'm a monster of ill-temper.'

'Funny I didn't notice that at the start.'

'I was pretending, in order to fool you because I needed a cheap room. Now I'm reverting to my true nature. Just wait and see.'

'Oh, you're impossible. I can't talk to you when you're in this mood.'

'Well, you don't need to talk to me,' Gino pointed out. 'Your prince has arrived, ten minutes late and looking anxious, as he ought.'

'I'll thump you in a minute.'

'Not you. It would disarrange your hair. Have a wonderful evening.'

She laughed and kissed his cheek, then ran across the road to where Steve's sleek car had drawn up.

'Hm!' said a voice at Gino's side.

'Hello, Tess. I didn't see you there.'

'Obviously. Very interesting, that was. Perhaps I should go away again.'

'Meaning? Meaning?'

'You and her.' Tess folded her arms and looked up

at him, teasing. 'You should have warned me you were in love.'

'What are you talking about?'

'I was watching you. You were a having a jealous fit.'

'That is my landlady,' he said in a repressive voice.

'So she may be, but you were still having a jealous fit.'

Gino breathed hard. 'Come into the pub and we'll have a long talk. It's time we got your love life back on track.'

'I think your love life's more interesting,' she said cheekily.

'I don't have a love life.'

'Well, that's not how it looked—'

'Let's get inside. I need a drink.'

He spoke edgily, for he was beginning to wonder how much more of Tess's company he would have to endure.

In the event his sufferings were short-lived. That evening Perry decided to assert himself. He stormed into the pub threatening dire retribution if 'this sort of thing' didn't stop at once.

Gino meekly agreed that 'this sort of thing' had gone on long enough, and retired from the field, leaving Perry triumphant and Tess ecstatic.

He could have gone straight home, but instead he set out in the other direction. By the time he returned home he'd walked five miles.

There was no sign of Laura, but he hadn't really expected that. Steve Deyton looked the kind of man who knew how to give a woman a good time, especially one who was so starved of a good time as Laura, he thought with a kind of rage.

Just why this should make him furious he wasn't quite sure, but she was vulnerable and Nikki was vulnerable and, as a good brother and uncle, he was going to watch out for them both.

He decided to be sensible and go to bed. But however hard he tried to sleep, one ear insisted on staying awake, listening for the sound of a car. And at last he heard one draw up outside.

He fought temptation for a good two seconds before sliding out of bed to go and stand at the window.

Steve Deyton had just switched the light on inside the car and Gino could clearly see him, talking to Laura. She showed no hurry to get out, but stayed there, leaning back against her seat, listening to him. She looked relaxed and beautiful.

Then Steve drew her to him and kissed her on the mouth. Laura laid her hand on his shoulder, not clasping him but not pushing him away either, then sliding her hand up to touch Steve's cheek lightly.

When they drew apart she was smiling. Through the glass Gino saw them bid each other goodnight, then Laura got out of the car and stood on the pavement until it had driven away.

Gino returned to bed and lay down, looking up at the ceiling, trying to wipe the pictures from his inner eye.

He heard the front door open and close. Then silence. At last he gave up the battle, pulled on a dressing gown and went down, making no sound with his bare feet. Laura didn't hear him. So he was able to see her while she was unaware.

She was in the living room, stretched out on the sofa, her hands clasped behind her head. Only one small lamp was on, and by its restricted light he thought he could see her eyes shining.

She had passed into a happy dream world, where everything was perfect. Her smile left no doubt about it. He wondered what had happened to make her smile that way.

As he watched she closed her eyes and gave a long, blissful sigh. He hesitated, undecided whether to go or stay, until she opened her eyes again and looked straight at him.

'Hello!' she said. 'Don't tell me you've been waiting up for me like my father?'

'Like your brother. Did you have a good time?'

'Mmmm!' she said, closing her eyes again.

He wished she wouldn't do that.

'So tell me about it. Where did you go?'

'To a nightclub. We had a wonderful dinner, and then we danced.'

'Till the dawn, Cinderella.'

She checked her watch. 'So it is. Never mind. I can't remember the last time I danced until dawn.'

'Are you seeing him again?'

'Stop sounding like a maiden aunt.'

'Meaning that you are?'

'Yes, if you must know. Oh, Gino, I like him so much. He's easy to talk to, and we just understand each other about everything. He told me about his wife, and how he felt when she died, and he has two children of his own, a girl and a boy.'

'Did you tell him about Nikki?'

'He knows I've got a daughter. No, I haven't told him everything. I've got to pick the right moment, because it has to be right for Nikki before I could even think of—well—'

'*Marrying him?*'

'That's a long way down the track.'

'It's not that far if you're thinking about it now.'

'No, I suppose not. The thing is—I know it's going to be all right. His son is a little disabled, something wrong with his spine, I think. So you see, I can rely on him to do and say the right things for Nikki, and when the time is right I'll introduce them.'

She saw him frowning and seized his hands.

'Oh, Gino, be happy for me. I've been so lonely, and if this works out I need never be lonely again. He's a good, kind man, and I may never get another chance.'

'Of course I'll be happy for you,' he said gruffly. 'If you're sure about this. I mean, so far it's just been one date.'

'I know. I'm not going to rush it. But it means so much to know that I have something to hope for.'

The wistfulness in her voice made him stop short. He couldn't say anything else.

Laura yawned and stretched.

'Ah, well, time for Cinderella to put away the glass slippers and get back to the kitchen.'

'Shall I make you some tea to bring you down to earth?' he asked, reaching out a hand to help her to her feet.

'No, thank you. I don't really want to come down too soon.'

She began to float around the room, whirling in time to unheard music, until she whirled a little too fast and swayed. She would have fallen if Gino hadn't caught her.

He clasped his hands behind her back, steadying her against his body. She held his shoulders, still in her blissful dream.

She felt good, a slim, lovely young woman, warm, vibrant and pressed against his body. At one time he would have known exactly what to do next: the bodies pressed together, the long, gentle kiss, the lips caressing, tentative at first, then urgent, demanding, then carry through to the inevitable end.

But now he couldn't do it. She was on a 'high' and she trusted him not to do what his senses were urging.

He couldn't betray a trust. Not with Alex. Not with Laura.

'Hey,' he said gently. 'The clock's struck twelve.'

'I want to stay in the ballroom for just a little longer,' she whispered.

'With Prince Steve Charming?' he asked ironically. 'And his big feet?'

'Oh, don't be unkind,' she murmured. 'He only trod on me twice.'

Gino gave a grunt of laughter. She too began to laugh, and he drew her close, wrapping his arms about her in a big hug.

'Come on, Cinders,' he said, drawing her out of the room and up the stairs.

Arms around each other's waist they made their way along the corridor to her door.

'Thanks, I'm all right now,' she said, opening the door. 'Hey, what are you doing?'

Gino had edged past her into the room and gone to her bedside table, where he took possession of her alarm clock.

'I'll cook breakfast tomorrow,' he said. 'You sleep late. Goodnight.'

He was as good as his word, rising at seven next morning and creeping downstairs to start work.

After half an hour Nikki crept in, and they both put their fingers to their lips, like conspirators.

Gino poured a cup of tea.

'Take this up to Mummy,' he said, 'and tell her to stay where she is. Those are my orders.'

Nikki giggled and went carefully upstairs. After a moment she returned and said, 'Mummy says you're a rotten bully and the worst man in the world. And thank you for the lovely tea.'

It was all right. He was her brother again. But it had been a near thing.

Like many factories Compulor did not stagger its holidays, but simply closed down, forcing everyone to take their holidays at the same time. Sadie and Claudia took a trip to France, and Gino found himself with nothing to do but laze around the house.

Nikki's school was out for the summer, and the two of them were thrown into each other's company.

'You don't have to let her monopolise every moment of your time,' Laura said guiltily. 'Even I can see that she's becoming a proper little tyrant.'

'I don't mind,' he said easily.

'It's nice of you to say so, but you have your own life to live.'

He gave his charming shrug as if to say, 'Do I?'

'Nikki bullies you.'

'Some men are just easily bullied.'

She surveyed him, her head on one side. 'You don't fool me.'

'Hm?' he said, wide-eyed.

'And don't give me that innocent look, because it doesn't work.'

'It does,' he insisted.

'No, it *used* to work, but I'm learning now, so stop your nonsense.'

'My nonsense? Please? *Non capisco*. Me no spikka da English.'

She chucked a cushion at him. 'You spikka da English perfectly well when you want to. You understand what suits you and you play dumb when it suits you.'

'Well, you get to learn a lot that way,' he conceded.

'"Easily bullied," my foot! I'll bet you can be as stubborn as a mule.'

'I can, but it's mostly pointless. I like a quiet life.'

'No, you don't,' she said suddenly. 'You've *settled* for a quiet life, but that's not the same thing.'

He was silent for a moment. 'You're very astute.'

'Gino,' she said impulsively, 'what is it that you do want? If you could have your perfect life, what would it be?'

'Oh—I don't know—' he murmured.

She caught a look on his face that had never been there before. Tension, wistfulness, desolation, they were all there, and for a moment she thought he would answer. But then the look was gone, leaving only blandness behind.

'If all your dreams came true,' she persisted, 'what would they be?'

'That's not the point of dreams,' he said.

'What do you mean?'

'Dreams aren't for coming true, they're for dreaming. If they come true you've lost them, and you have to find another dream.'

'But that's not what happened to you, is it?' she asked. 'You didn't get what you dreamed of.'

He smiled at her but he was looking into the distance.

'Maybe the things I dreamed about were things I had no right to,' he said.

'But they were still your dreams. Were they beautiful?'

'Yes, they were beautiful,' he said softly. 'But forbidden, although I didn't know it then. I know it now.'

'Aren't there other things to dream of?' she asked quietly.

He shook his head. 'It's better not to. You just end up wasting a lot of time. You asked about my ideal life. I suppose it would be much like the one I have.'

So he wasn't going to let her in, she thought. Tonight he'd let her creep nearer to his confidence than ever before, but even so the door had swung shut at the last minute, leaving her with the frustrating feeling that Gino was like an iceberg. Not in his nature, for a more warm-hearted, sweet-tempered man never lived, but in the way he concealed nine-tenths of himself beneath a smiling surface.

CHAPTER SIX

GINO was getting used to hearing Steve's car draw up late at night, then pause, then the front door. He no longer went to the window, but sometimes he would join Laura in the kitchen afterwards, trying to read the progress of the relationship in her face.

He knew he should be glad for her, since she seemed to have found the ideal man, but he couldn't make himself do it. Trying to analyse his unease was frustrating, because the best he could come up with was that Steve bore a marked resemblance to Laura's ex-husband. And that made him more uneasy than ever.

One night, after she had returned, he emerged into the dark corridor in time to hear Laura and Nikki talking in the child's room.

'Go to sleep, now,' he heard Laura say from the door.

'But you did have a lovely time, didn't you, Mummy?'

'Yes, I did, and it's time you were asleep.'

'But—'

'Goodnight,' Laura said, laughing but firm as she closed the door.

'She's a little monkey,' Gino observed as they went downstairs together.

In the kitchen they settled down to have one of their late-night chats over a cup of tea. Gino wondered how many more times this would happen.

'You're bursting with news,' he said, looking at her glowing face.

'I told him about Nikki. Everything's wonderful.'

Something hit him in the stomach. 'That's great.'

'He was so supportive and understanding. Oh, Gino, I'm so happy—'

The doorbell rang.

'Who's that at this hour?' Gino muttered, rising and making his way towards the door.

Afterwards he realised that he should have guessed, or at least been on the alert. But he was off guard, and it came as a total surprise when he opened the door and saw Steve Deyton.

'Hi!' Steve said cheerily. 'You must be Gino. Laura's told me about you.'

He grasped Gino's hand and pumped it up and down, while contriving to slip past him into the hall.

'Laura left her scarf in the car,' he said, 'so I thought I'd bring it back. Hello, darling!'

This was to Laura who'd come out into the hall, smiling as she saw him, opening her arms to be enclosed in his.

Then it happened.

There was the sound of footsteps scampering downstairs, an eager cry of—

'Mummy, is that—?'

Steve, facing the stairs, raised his eyes and caught his first glimpse of Nikki. Time seemed to stop. From where he was standing Gino saw everything in his face, the frozen shock, the horror, the revulsion.

What broke Gino's heart was that Nikki saw it too.

Laura, facing the other direction, didn't know what was happening. But she heard Nikki check, felt Steve grow tense, and drew back to look at his face, just in time to see him adjust his expression.

She knew at once. She'd seen that hasty adjustment too often to be mistaken about it. She stepped back from him as though he were poison.

Incredibly, Gino thought, the only one not stunned to silence was Nikki. She descended the last stairs and came forward to Steve.

'Hello,' she said calmly. 'I'm Nikki.'

'Hello, Nikki,' he said mechanically.

His eyes moved from side to side like a man desperately seeking a way out. Nikki, watching him, knew everything.

She took a step closer to Gino. Her hand slipped into his and squeezed it hard. He squeezed back.

'What are you doing down here you rascal?' Gino asked, hoping his voice didn't shake. 'You were supposed to be asleep ages ago. Come on. Upstairs with you.'

Without a word she went with him. Hand in hand they went up together, and along to her room. Nikki kept a tight hold of his hand until she was in bed and he was tucking her up.

They looked at each other. There was a calm determination about the child that he had to respect, and no way was he going to insult her with comforting platitudes that she was too intelligent to believe.

'He isn't magic, like you,' she said at last in a voice that was too grim for a child.

'I guess not everyone can be magic,' he said gently. 'Maybe we should feel sorry for people who aren't. They're not special, like us.'

She nodded.

'I suppose you meet a lot like him,' he ventured.

'Yes. I don't really mind—' her voice wobbled.

Gino abandoned words and enfolded her in a bear hug. They were sitting like that when Laura came in. Her face was tight, angry, and she looked as if she'd been crying.

'Here's Mummy,' Gino said softly.

There was no movement from Nikki.

'Nikki?' he whispered, leaning over slightly, trying to see her face.

Still there was no answer, except her deep, regular breathing.

'She's gone to sleep,' he said.

Gently they lowered Nikki back onto the pillows. Somehow she'd taken hold of Gino's hand again and he had to ease away carefully. But he managed it without waking her, and they crept out of the room.

'Are you all right?' he asked.

'I will be.'

'Come here,' he said, opening his own door and showing her in. 'You need some of this.'

From his wardrobe he took out a bottle of Chianti and opened it.

'I bought it because I was feeling homesick,' he said, producing a glass and filling it. 'Drink. It'll do you more good than all the words in the world.'

Laura sat on the edge of the bed, which was almost the only place to sit, and sipped the wine.

'It's good. And who needs words anyway? It was all over as soon as I saw his face.'

'You wouldn't marry him now?'

'Not in a million years, not after he hurt her. But he wouldn't ask me now, I know that.'

'What happened after I left?'

'He was embarrassed. He kept giving this little nervous giggle and he couldn't meet my eyes. We were supposed to be going out on Friday, but he'd suddenly remembered that there might be a problem about that.'

'Oh, yeah?' Gino asked cynically.

'Yeah,' she echoed with a little wry smile.

'Then he said he'd call me to arrange something else. He won't of course. It's over. How could I have got him so wrong?'

'I guess you wanted to believe in him.'

'Yes, I wanted it too much. I was a fool.'

'You're not a fool just because you want to feel loved and wanted. It's what we all want.'

'But I have no right to want it,' she said. 'I shouldn't have let myself forget that. I can't take my happiness at Nikki's expense.'

'There wouldn't have been any happiness, not with him.'

'You were right about him. Now you can say I told you so.'

'Do you think I will?'

'No, you're too good a friend for that.'

'Laura,' he asked hesitantly, 'were you very much in love with him?'

She was silent a long time.

'I don't know,' she said at last. 'I thought I was. Now I'm just full of anger and bitterness towards him for reacting like that. If he hadn't—I don't know. What's the point of talking about it now?'

She finished with a disconsolate sigh. Gino sat down beside her on the bed, and slipped his arm around her.

'You've still got your brother,' he said.

She gave a shaky laugh. 'Poor Gino. First Nikki, now me. You ought to set up as an agony aunt.'

'I'm not "poor Gino" and I'd rather you turn to me than anyone else. More Chianti?'

'I'd better not. I'm going to bed now.'

'You'll feel better in the morning,' he said, wishing he felt more sure of that. 'Come along, I'll walk you home.'

He escorted her solemnly along the corridor, and opened her bedroom door.

'Thank goodness you were there,' she mused. 'It would have been much worse for Nikki otherwise. Goodnight, Gino.'

'Goodnight.'

When she had closed the door he hesitated, wondering whether to go away or knock and give her another chance to talk.

After a while he heard the sound of weeping. And then he knew that he had no place here.

As Laura had predicted, Steve did not call her. Nor did he come into the pub again. He was allowed to fade into the past, and never mentioned by any of them.

Gino fell into the habit of dropping into The Running Sheep just in time for one drink before Laura was ready to leave. She never had to walk home alone.

'Thank you,' she said one night.

'What for?'

'Everything,' she said simply.

When they'd walked a little further she asked, 'What happened to your girlfriend, the one with the voluptuous figure.'

'She found a better man. I left the field in defeat.'

'You mean you dumped her?'

'Certainly not,' he said, shocked. 'I'm a gentleman. I never dump a lady. I let her dump me.'

She shot him a sideways glance. As she'd guessed, he was grinning.

When they got in there was a message waiting for her by the phone. *Call Mark.*

'Mark?' Gino queried.

'Just a friend,' Laura said vaguely. 'Why don't you go and put the kettle on?'

'You'll make an Englishman of me yet,' he predicted, and headed for the kitchen.

She joined him a few minutes later and announced that she would have to be out the next evening too, although not at the pub.

'You've got a date,' Gino said.

'No, of course not. I just—have to be out.'

'With Mark.'

'Stop fishing and pour me some tea. Mrs Baxter, you'll be in tomorrow night, won't you?'

'Yes, I'll be here. Gino and I will look after Nikki so you'll be all right, *wherever you're going.*'

'That's lovely,' Laura said brightly. 'Goodnight, you two.'

She left them and went upstairs. Mrs Baxter muttered, 'It's always the same. Mark rings. She drops everything to go out, and won't tell anyone where she's going.'

'A woman of mystery,' Gino mused.

'I'll say. And it's no use asking her, because she just clams up.'

He discovered that this was true. For some reason he felt piqued by Laura's determination to keep the secret from him.

'I'll drive you there,' he offered when she was ready to go the next evening.

'No thanks, I can drive myself.'

'Suppose there's an emergency? How do I contact you?'

'On my mobile.'

'You're being very annoying, you know that?'

'Goodnight, Gino.'

Laura picked up a small bag that she'd set waiting in

the hall, and whisked herself off, leaving him staring at the front door, speechless.

'Claudia and Sadie are coming home from holiday tonight,' Nikki said.

'Not till the early hours,' Mrs Baxter reminded her.

'And then it's back to work to the stresses and strains of the packing department,' Gino mused. 'I don't know how I'll stand the excitement. Good heavens! Whatever's that?'

'It's a nut cake,' Mrs Baxter said, producing it from a cupboard. 'I bought it this afternoon, for everyone.'

'It's made with lots and lots of different kinds of nuts,' Nikki assured him. 'It's gorgeous.'

It was a pleasant evening. Mrs Baxter was an army widow who had travelled extensively, and had a fund of funny stories. But when she had told a few of them she said, 'Of course the best thing of all is my family. I'm going to become a grandmother some time next month. I'm so looking forward to that.'

She glanced at Nikki, who had begun to yawn. 'I think it's time you went to bed, don't you?'

Nikki nodded and agreed without argument. When she'd gone Mrs Baxter produced a bottle of sherry.

'You haven't eaten your cake yet,' she told Gino.

'I've been too busy laughing at your stories. Don't you have any more?'

Before Mrs Baxter could speak the phone rang. She answered it, and Gino saw her turn pale.

'Yes—yes—I'll be there as quickly as I can,' she assured someone.

'What is it?' he asked when she'd hung up.

'That was my son. My daughter-in-law has gone into labour a month early, and there are complications. Oh, dear, I need to go to them as soon as possible.'

'I'll call you a taxi while you pack,' he said at once. 'And I'll stay here, so Nikki can't come to any harm.'

The taxi arrived a few minutes later. Gino saw Mrs Baxter into it and waved her off with many expressions of good luck.

Now he could he settle down with his uneaten slice of nut cake. It was delicious. After arguing with his conscience for a moment he decided that he could easily buy another cake for the others, and cut himself a second slice. It was as delicious as the first.

As he mulled over the thought of a third slice, he became aware that something strange was happening. The cake had started to move. Before his eyes it grew larger, then smaller. He reached out to touch it, but it wasn't where it ought to have been.

A feeling of nausea attacked him. His head was swelling like a balloon, while his throat became tighter.

He couldn't breathe. Struggling to his feet, he kicked the chair over. He fought for air but only managed to make a horrible noise, and tearing open his shirt gave him no relief. The tightness was inside. Iron fingers seemed to grip his throat as though someone was intent on choking the life out of him.

He wasn't aware of falling but he knew he must have done when his head hit the floor. Half in and half out of consciousness, he saw the furniture looming over him, menacing.

He must reach the telephone in the hall and call for help. But there were lead weights on his limbs and it was a huge effort to move them. Slowly he dragged himself an inch forward, then another inch. The pounding in his head grew louder, like a drum banging.

He knew now that he was dying.

Blackness swamped him, he didn't know how long for. He was partly drawn back by a scream.

'Daddy, Daddy!'

Someone was shaking him. The mist cleared a little, just enough for him to make out a pink rabbit. He stared, trying to make some sense of it, then of the blue rabbit that appeared beside it.

'Daddy!'

Nikki's face appeared, frantic and tearful. The rabbits were on her pyjamas, he remembered. Yes, that was it. But why was she here when she should be upstairs, asleep? Laura would be annoyed that he wasn't doing a better job of babysitting, but he wasn't going to see Laura again. He was dying. He knew that.

Then he lost sight of her, but he could still hear her from the hall, screaming, *'Ambulance! My daddy's dying—'*

With every moment it grew harder to breathe. It would be over soon. But Nikki was there again, plumping down on the floor beside him, crying to him.

'They're on their way, but they say you've got to be calm—if you fight for breath it gets harder. Try to be calm slowly—slowly—slowly—'

She wasn't making any sense. He couldn't breathe at all, never mind slowly. But gradually her voice seemed to penetrate his subconscious. Without meaning to, he ceased fighting and lay, his eyes on her, feeling the world slip away from him.

In the distance a bell shrilled—voices—strangers wearing green and yellow coming into the kitchen, kneeling beside him, Nikki talking through her tears. Someone fitted an oxygen mask over his face, and then he really did pass out.

*　　*　　*

Laura, returning home, found the house empty and a note on the kitchen table. Printed across the top was the word *Paramedics*. It said, 'Your husband collapsed and was taken to Canning Hospital. Your daughter came with him.'

The roads were quiet and even in the cranky old car she made the hospital in a few minutes. Entering the Emergency department she saw Nikki almost at once. The little girl threw herself into her mother's arms, sobbing wildly.

'What's happened?' she asked tensely.

'We're not quite certain yet,' a tired young woman doctor told her, 'but your husband may have a nut allergy.

'My—?'

'Could you let us know his name? Your little girl just said "Daddy" when she called the ambulance.'

'You did that?' she looked at Nikki.

'I woke up. There was a noise downstairs, a big clatter, and I went down. He was on the floor, choking, and he was a terrible colour—'

'So she did exactly the right thing and called the ambulance,' the doctor said. 'Almost certainly saved his life. His throat swelled up so much that he was choking to death.'

'The woman on the phone said I should try to calm him down,' Nikki said, 'and I did try, but I don't know if it worked.'

'The paramedics seem to think that it did,' said the doctor. 'You helped him a lot. We've inserted a tube into his windpipe and he's breathing through that at the moment.'

'Is he going to be all right?' Laura asked in alarm.

'I think so. I've given him an injection and it seems to be working. It would help if I knew the precise nature of the allergy.'

'But I don't know—' she faltered.

'He was eating the nut cake, Mummy,' Nikki explained. 'I know because he still had a bit in his hand, and there's lots of different nuts in it.'

'And he wouldn't have started it if he'd known he was allergic,' Laura said. 'So there must have been something in there he'd never had before.'

'Could I have his name please?'

'Gino Farnese,' she said in a daze. 'Can I see him?'

'Yes, of course, but I'm not sure that your little girl should see him as he is. He doesn't look very nice right now.'

At these words Nikki clutched her mother more tightly, and her mouth set in mulish lines.

'I'm sure he doesn't,' Laura said. 'But I guess he must have looked pretty scary when he collapsed. Nikki didn't lose her head, and I think she needs to see that he's still with us.'

Despite her resolute words Laura almost cried out at the sight of Gino lying in the hospital bed. His face was still swollen and the tube in his neck looked brutal, although she knew it was keeping him alive. She bit her lips to keep back her emotion.

At that moment Gino opened his eyes and saw them. His swollen mouth moved in an attempt at speech.

'Don't talk,' she said urgently. 'I know everything that happened. Nikki told me.'

'Mrs Baxter,' he mouthed. 'Baby—early—'

'Her first grandchild is due,' Laura remembered. 'It came early? She had to go?'

By the way he relaxed she knew she'd got it right.

'Nikki—' His lips shaped Nikki's name.

'She found you and called the ambulance.'

'Said—keep—calm—'

Gino's eyes closed. He looked as if the effort had exhausted him.

Nikki climbed into Laura's lap, and the two of them sat, arms entwined, silently watching the bed. Now that the first shock was abating, the place where it had been was filling up with horror as she realised how close to death Gino had come.

And it had happened without warning, out of the blue, because of a weakness he had never known that he had. Nothing and nobody was safe, she brooded. Life could snatch everything from you, just like that.

'Is he really going to be all right?' she asked a nurse who came in to glance at some charts.

'His results are getting better all the time. The swelling's going down and we'll be able to take the tube out soon.'

'Then I'll come back tomorrow.'

'Oh, no, Mummy—' Nikki was up in arms at the thought that Gino could survive without her protection.

'We must go home, darling.'

'But he might die if we're not here,' Nikki sobbed.

'No.' It was a croak from the bed. Gino's head was turned towards Nikki. 'Not die,' he whispered. 'Because—of—you.'

'He needs to sleep,' Laura told Nikki. 'We'll come back tomorrow.'

But Nikki had one more thing to do before she was ready to leave. Carefully negotiating the tubes she edged forward and kissed Gino's cheek.

''Night,' she said.

''Night,' he murmured.

He closed his eyes. When he opened them again the nurse was still there, but the other two had gone. She glanced up and smiled at him.

'Your daughter's a real character,' she said. 'You must be very proud of her.'

Your daughter. He frowned, wondering if the nurse had really said that, but he was too tired to think about it. He drifted into an unquiet dream.

They found Sadie and Claudia at home, having arrived so recently that they were still in their outdoor clothes.

'We couldn't think why the house was dark and empty,' Sadie said. 'Where did everyone vanish to?'

Laura told the story and they exclaimed over Gino's misfortune and Nikki's quick thinking.

'But now it's time to go back to bed,' Laura said. 'It's two in the morning.'

As she got into bed Nikki said, 'He is going to be all right, isn't he?'

'He is, now,' Laura said, tucking her in. 'Darling, did you really tell them he was your daddy?'

'I suppose so. I just said the first thing that came into my head, about how he was choking to death, and our address. I didn't think much about the rest.'

'Darling, please don't think of Gino as your father.'

'It's just—wouldn't it be nice if—?'

Laura's heart ached for her daughter, to whom life never gave anything she wanted.

'It can't happen, pet. Please don't think about it.'

'But he's special,' Nikki insisted.

'Yes, he is. Very special. I know he's your best friend—'

'And yours too.'

'And mine too. I hope he always will be, but he doesn't belong to us, and he never can.'

Nikki didn't argue further. At nine she could accept disappointment without rebellion, being so used to it.

She snuggled down and gave her mother a smile.

'It would have been nice, though,' she said, and closed her eyes.

'Yes,' Laura whispered. 'It would.'

She held Nikki's hand until the child fell asleep. As she slipped out of the room she heard the phone going in the hall downstairs.

She found Claudia taking the call, looking shocked.

'It's the hospital,' she said. 'They seem to think you're Gino's wife and they want you to go back as fast as you can. He's taken a sudden turn for the worse, and they're really worried.'

CHAPTER SEVEN

IT WAS good to be home. He'd missed the crimson sunsets and glowing colours of Tuscany. Even more, he'd missed the loving family that had always been his. His father, bellowing, jovial, mischievous, infinitely loving. And his brother Rinaldo, gruff, unyielding, withdrawn, but with a fierce power of love that had equalled their father's.

Why had he left them?

Then he realised that nothing was quite as he remembered. He'd meant to come home, but home no longer existed. Where was his father? He looked around him for the farmhouse he loved, with its two incongruous flights of stone steps up the front.

But the landscape was a desert, and in the centre, strangely, was a funeral.

There was Rinaldo, his face full of rage and hostility. Why? And the fair-haired woman, watching them both across the open grave. Who was she? Surely he should know her? But there was a mystery about her that he couldn't unravel.

Agitated voices reached him out of the mists. *'His temperature's shooting up again. We have to get it down fast. This wasn't supposed to happen.'*

No, it hadn't been supposed to happen. He shouldn't have fallen in love with Alex, because when they tossed a coin for her, Rinaldo had won. But he hadn't wanted her, until it was too late for all of them and disaster had been inevitable.

Now he knew the woman watching them across the grave with cool, appraising eyes. She was Alex who had lit up his life and then left him desolate.

He and Alex had spent the first day of her trip together. He'd shown her the city of Florence, and then they'd driven out into the country to hire riding horses. That was how he remembered her best, laughing as she rode beside him through the sunlight.

He could feel that sunlight on him now, fierce, blazing, almost unbearably hot. She had flowered in that heat, becoming a woman of Italy, discovering that she belonged there.

He'd known then that he loved her, not like his other 'light o'loves', but finally, completely, with a total giving of himself, nothing held back. That was something he'd never felt able to do before, and it had fulfilled him.

After that there could be no other woman but her, and the knowledge filled him with joy. He'd seen that joy mirrored in her—or so he'd thought until the moment he found them together in Rinaldo's bed, folded in each other's arms.

He tried to shy away from that memory. It brought too much pain. But his mind insisted on forcing him to confront it, as though it was trying to convey an urgent message.

He saw them again, naked limbs entwined, lost in each other, and he knew there was something here that he'd failed to understand, but which he *must* understand if he were ever again to know peace.

There was her face again, blurred this time, but he could see that she was gazing at him sadly, anxiously. She'd looked like that at their last meeting, not the day of her wedding to Rinaldo, but before that, when they'd spoken alone, face to face, for the last time.

'Be damned to the pair of you!' he'd cried in his anguish, although she'd tried to make him understand that she hadn't taken him seriously, had thought he was only playing at love. And it had been true to start with.

'But then I found I was really in love with you.'

That was what he'd told her, and now he tried to say it again through parched, swollen lips. He wanted to make her understand.

'Gino—Gino—' Her voice reached him down long, echoing corridors.

'Carissima—'

'Gino try to wake up—look at me, *please*—'

'I always loved—to look at you,' he told her sadly. 'Do you remember—that day in the barn, you were so beautiful—'

She was silent, but he could still feel her hands holding his.

'I wanted to take you in my arms,' he murmured. 'I loved you so much.'

'Did you?' she whispered.

He thought she sounded almost wistful, but that must be part of his fevered madness.

'You never knew,' he murmured, 'but I woke up thinking about you and went to bed thinking about you. Such dreams of you I had—I'd be ashamed to tell you—'

'You could tell me now,' she said softly.

'You would be angry with me. I dreamed of holding you in my arms when we were naked—we made love— I had no right to think of you that way—'

'Right has nothing to do with it,' she said gently. 'You love whom you love.'

GET FREE BOOKS and a FREE GIFT WHEN YOU PLAY THE...

Lucky 7

Just scratch off the silver box with a coin. Then check below to see the gifts you get!

SLOT MACHINE GAME!

YES! I have scratched off the silver box. Please send me the 2 free Harlequin Romance® books and gift for which I qualify. I understand I am under no obligation to purchase any books, as explained on the back of this card.

386 HDL D2AQ   **186 HDL D33W**

FIRST NAME   LAST NAME

ADDRESS

APT.#   CITY

STATE/PROV.   ZIP/POSTAL CODE

7	7	7	**Worth TWO FREE BOOKS plus a BONUS Mystery Gift!**
🍒	🍒	🍒	**Worth TWO FREE BOOKS!**
♣	♣	♣	**Worth ONE FREE BOOK!**
🔔	🔔	🍒	**TRY AGAIN!**

www.eHarlequin.com

(H-R-08/04)

DETACH AND MAIL CARD TODAY!

The Harlequin Reader Service® — Here's how it works:

Accepting your 2 free books and gift places you under no obligation to buy anything. You may keep the books and gift and return the shipping statement marked "cancel." If you do not cancel, about a month later we'll send you 6 additional books and bill you just $3.57 each in the U.S., or $4.05 each in Canada, plus 25¢ shipping & handling per book and applicable taxes if any.* That's the complete price and — compared to cover prices of $4.25 each in the U.S. and $4.99 each in Canada — it's quite a bargain! You may cancel at any time, but if you choose to continue, every month we'll send you 6 more books, which you may either purchase at the discount price or return to us and cancel your subscription. *Terms and prices subject to change without notice. Sales tax applicable in N.Y. Canadian residents will be charged applicable provincial taxes and GST. Credit or debit balances in a customer's account(s) may be offset by any other outstanding balance owed by or to the customer.

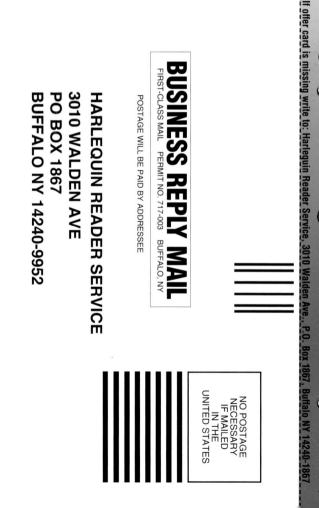

If offer card is missing write to: Harlequin Reader Service, 3010 Walden Ave., P.O. Box 1867, Buffalo NY 14240-1867

BUSINESS REPLY MAIL
FIRST-CLASS MAIL   PERMIT NO. 717-003   BUFFALO, NY

POSTAGE WILL BE PAID BY ADDRESSEE

HARLEQUIN READER SERVICE
3010 WALDEN AVE
PO BOX 1867
BUFFALO NY 14240-9952

NO POSTAGE
NECESSARY
IF MAILED
IN THE
UNITED STATES

'That's true. I couldn't help loving you and I wanted everything with you. And when I held you, you were beautiful—as beautiful as I always knew you would be. And I told you that you were my love, for ever. I know I must never say that again, only think it. I can't spend my life with you, but I can spend my life loving you.'

Through the mist he saw her shake her head.

'That's a long time,' she said. 'Time to forget and love again.'

His hands moved, holding hers.

'You don't understand. Why should I want to love again when I've found the perfect woman?'

'No woman is perfect,' she insisted, and he had the strange feeling that she was pleading with him. 'There's always someone else, who might be even better—'

'Not for me.'

'But suppose she loved you? Don't you want to *be* loved as well as to give love—?'

'Yes,' he whispered, 'I wanted that.'

'Wouldn't that be better than wasting your life on something that's hopeless?'

'Much better—common sense. But—not for me.'

He tightened his hand on hers, drawing it slowly up to his mouth so that his lips could lie against it.

'*Amor mio,*' he whispered. '*Per tutta la vita.*'

Her hand vanished as though she'd snatched it back. In the same moment her blurred face melted away, and he was alone in the burning darkness again.

It swirled around him, tossing him about violently, like a whirlwind. He tried to touch ground, but there was no ground, nothing to hold onto, no safety, no joy, only a world of fearsome nothingness.

Gradually the heat began to abate. The glowing Tuscan colours faded into hospital pastels, reality shud-

dered back into place, and he awoke to find himself in
a cold world.

He saw the end of the bed, the pale green walls, and
a mass of bleeping machinery. His neck hurt, but he
managed to turn his head slowly, and saw Laura standing by the window, looking out.

'Hello,' he managed to say. The tube was gone from
his neck but he was still hoarse.

She turned and smiled quickly, but her face was pale
and distraught.

'Hello,' she said in a strained voice. 'I'll fetch someone.'

She left the room before he could speak, and from
the corridor he heard her say, 'He's come round.'

There were footsteps, a nurse appearing, smiling with
relief. 'That's better,' she said. 'You gave us a fright.'

'Why, what happened?'

'Just when we thought you were on the mend you
took a bad turn. Your temperature shot right up again,
and we called your wife back quickly, just in case. Let
me check your temperature, although I can see it's well
down. Yes—that's normal.'

After a few more checks the nurse left them. Gino
wondered why Laura was keeping back from him, near
the window.

'Have you been with me all the time?' he asked.

'Most of it. They sent for me last night because Nikki
said—er—she said you were her daddy, and they as-
sumed we were either married or—'

'Uh-huh! I guessed that.'

'I didn't tell them otherwise because if they think I'm
your next of kin it makes things easier.'

'Right. I'm glad they sent for you. I wouldn't have
liked to die alone.'

'Gino, you're not going to die.'

'Not now. But I know how close to it I came.'

Laura nodded. 'Yes, it got very scary. Would you like me to contact your family? After all, I'm *not* your next of kin, and maybe they should know?'

He was silent.

'Give me a number to call,' she suggested.

'There's no need,' he said at last. 'I'm past the worst now.'

'But suppose you *had* died? How would I get in touch with them?'

'There's an address book in my room, but don't use it now. I'm getting better and there's no need.' His voice was weak, but he spoke with a firmness that told her the subject was closed.

'As you wish,' she said. 'How are you feeling?'

'Dreadful. My throat feels as though I've swallowed thorns, and my brain is off the planet. I'm so light-headed I'm floating between two worlds.'

'You had a terrible fever. You were delirious.'

'Did I talk much?' He didn't look at her as he spoke.

'A bit, but don't ask me what you said. It was in Italian.'

She saw that some of his tension eased.

'Was it all in Italian?' he asked, as casually as he could. 'I didn't say anything I shouldn't, did I?'

'Not that I noticed.'

He gave her his winning smile. 'I just wondered if I'd offended you, and that was why you were keeping your distance.'

He stretched out his hand, and after a moment she came forward and took it, sitting carefully on the side of the bed.

'What time is it?' he asked.

'Seven in the morning. I'd like to be home before Nikki awakes, so that she doesn't need to know that I was ever away.'

'Right.' He tightened his hand. 'Poor Laura. I've kept you up all night, and now you've got to start a day's work. I'm sorry.'

'Not your fault,' she said gruffly.

'You must rue the day you ever met me.'

'You know I don't. If anything had happened to you—well—'

'Nikki,' he said, understanding. 'Well, tell Nikki I'm fine, thanks to her.'

'I will. Goodbye for now.'

She squeezed his hand and left him.

Laura just made it home before Nikki was up. In a low voice she outlined events to the others, who promised to say nothing. They were acting normally by the time Nikki came bounding downstairs, eager for news of Gino.

'We will go and see him tonight, won't we?' she demanded over breakfast. 'Otherwise he'll wonder what's happened to us.'

'We'll go,' Laura promised.

At last they all departed, Nikki and Mrs Baxter to school, Sadie and Claudia to the factory. Laura started the housework, but in Sadie's bedroom she stopped, fighting with her conscience.

Sadie possessed a state-of-the-art computer, bought at cost price from the factory. She'd shown Laura how to use it, and get online.

She did so now. Searching feverishly she found what she wanted, a website that did translations. With shaking hands she typed in *per tutta la vita*. She could remember the words clearly. They were burned into her brain.

The translation came up. For all my life.

Gino had said, *Amor mio, per tutta la vita.*

'My love, for all my life.'

But he had said it to Alex, not to her. She'd known that, even as he grasped her hands and babbled deliriously of love. None of it had been meant for herself. His eyes had been open but he'd seen only the woman he loved and always would, because no other woman existed for him. He'd poured out his heart to Alex in passionate words that she would never hear.

He'd spoken in a jumble of English and Italian. Laura hadn't understood it all, but she'd followed enough for her heart to ache for him. Of course, Gino was only her brother, but it had hurt her to the heart to see him lying there, perhaps dying, tortured by what he yearned for, and which could never be his.

Why had she spoken to him of a woman who might return his love? She hadn't meant to say it, but the words had spoken themselves without her willing them. Or so it had seemed.

She switched off the machine and returned to her work, but everything she did was mechanical as thoughts raged through her head.

By the end of the day they had resolved themselves into no conclusions, and somewhere in her breast was the dull ache of a heavy stone. Almost like grief.

When Laura had gone Gino lay still, troubled by a strange feeling that had come to him in the last few minutes. The sense of hovering between two worlds was back, stronger than ever, and it had to do with something that had happened in the last few minutes.

He fought to recall the memory, but it was elusive and the effort tired him.

For the rest of the day he slept in snatches between visits from doctors who changed his medication, said he was on the mend, but predicted that it would be several days before he was strong enough to leave.

All his life he had been physically strong, and now his own weakness maddened him. By evening he was exhausted, but he knew he must be at his best to ease Nikki's mind.

He managed to be out of bed, wrapped in a hospital towel dressing gown, a scarf around his throat to cover the wound, sitting in a chair, looking fairly normal.

When Nikki came through the door he put on a smile and opened his arms for her to run into them. Laura smiled at the sight and went to sit by the window.

'Are you really, really, really all right?' Nikki demanded.

'Really, really, really,' he confirmed.

'Look what I've brought you,' she said, diving into a plastic bag she was carrying.

It was Simon, the toy dog she'd given him on the first day.

'Nikki,' Laura protested, laughing, 'Gino can't have Simon beside him in hospital.'

'Yes, I can,' he said at once. 'He's my friend, because Nikki's my friend, and she gave him to me.'

He set the toy on the bedside table, which delighted Nikki. She began to chatter about her day, and he listened, quiet and contented, until Nikki said, 'Mummy, do you—?'

'Hush,' Gino said. 'I think she's asleep.'

Laura had slid down in her seat and was leaning against the wall, breathing deeply.

'Let her sleep,' Gino told Nikki. 'She works so hard.'

Nikki nodded. 'And she was crying today.'

'What?'

'When I got home she was in the kitchen. She came out quickly but I saw her put her handkerchief away, and her eyes were red.'

'Did she say anything to you?'

Nikki shook her head. 'Mummy never tells people about the times she cries.'

'I'm sure she doesn't,' Gino murmured. 'I don't suppose she tells anyone anything, really. Who can she talk to?'

'You. She tells you everything.'

Gino shook his head. 'No, she tells me a lot, but there's also a lot she feels she has to keep to herself.'

'But why doesn't she tell *you*?'

'It's not that easy, *piccina*. She's a very brave and a very lonely person. Let her sleep. I haven't thanked you yet for what you did. Tell me all about it.'

She complied happily, giving a graphic description of finding him lying on the floor choking to death. Gino was able to piece together his own fractured memories, and to realise again exactly how much he owed to her.

At last the nurse looked in to say that Visiting Time was almost over.

'Shall I wake Mummy?' Nikki asked.

'No, I'll do it.'

He began to ease himself up out of the chair, wobbled and clutched Nikki's shoulder to steady himself. Using her as a support he made his way across to Laura and sat down facing her.

'Laura,' he said gently shaking her shoulders.

She didn't wake. He looked closely at her face, seeing how white and tired she looked.

'Does she have to work tonight?' he asked Nikki quietly.

'No, we'll go straight home.'

'Good. Take care of her, Nikki. Make sure she goes to bed at once.'

Nikki nodded. 'Leave it to me,' she said solemnly.

'Laura,' he said again, touching her shoulder. 'Laura, wake up.'

She opened her eyes slowly, looking straight at him.

'Hello,' he said, smiling. 'Wake up. Nikki's going to take you home.'

'*She's* taking *me* home?'

'Yes, I told her to. She's going to look after you. Someone needs to.'

Laura got sleepily to her feet.

'Come along, Mummy,' Nikki said gravely.

Gino watched them go, then made his way slowly back to bed. He had a lot to think about.

The next evening it was Sadie who brought Nikki to the hospital.

'Mummy had to go out to work suddenly,' she explained.

'At The Running Sheep?'

'No, it's another one,' Sadie explained. 'It's owned by someone called Mark.'

'Oh, him!' Gino growled. 'Yes, I remember, he called the other night.'

'I don't think Laura's on the regular staff because he just calls up and books her for one stint. He called this morning and wanted her for tonight. It's unusual for him to want her for two bookings so close together.'

'What's the name of this other place?'

'I've no idea. Laura doesn't talk about it. Before I forget, everyone at the factory sends their good wishes,

and the chief packer says don't worry about your job,
which, considering you've been doing two men's work
for one man's wages isn't the biggest surprise in the
world.'

'Well, I'll be out of here soon.'

'But not fit for work, surely,' Sadie said, eyeing him.
'You're not going to regain your strength overnight. Or
even in a few days. You've been knocked for six.'

'Yes, I have,' he murmured. 'In many ways.'

Laura came in alone at lunchtime next day.

'Nikki's at school,' she said, 'and I wanted to see
you quickly to apologise about the other night. Coming
to see you, then nodding off.'

'You don't have to apologise for falling asleep,' Gino
said. 'Especially when you were up all night with me.
Between you and Nikki I'm piling up a huge debt.'

'I think we're just repaying our debt to you.'

He shook his head. 'She saved my life by acting so
fast. I made her tell me the details, and it's quite a story.
I must find a way to thank her for it. Do you know of
anything that she specially wants?'

It seemed to him that Laura took a long time to answer. 'Yes, I do.'

'Then tell me and it's hers.'

There was a strange note in Laura's voice as she said,
'It may not be that simple. Gino, just what would you
be prepared to do for Nikki?'

'For the person who saved my life? What wouldn't I
be prepared to do? Name it.'

'Give her what she wants most in the world.'

'But I don't know what that is.'

'Yes, you do,' Laura said with a hint of urgency in
her voice. 'She's told us in her own way, when she

called you Daddy. That's what she wants most, Gino. She wants you to be her father.'

'But how can I—?'

Laura took a deep breath. 'By marrying her mother. I'm asking you to marry me, Gino.'

As Gino stared at her, wondering if he'd heard properly, Laura said quickly, 'Don't say anything. Let me explain what I mean, first.'

'Explain?'

'What I have in mind needs some explaining. It wouldn't be real marriage, you see. In name only. You wouldn't be tied down. You could live just as you please, have girlfriends if you want, as long as Nikki didn't know. I wouldn't ask questions or get jealous.'

'It doesn't sound much of a deal for you.' He was speaking vaguely, trying to get his thoughts in order.

'All I ask is that you make Nikki happy,' she said. 'If you can do that, it's a wonderful deal for me. The best deal in the world.'

'Don't you want anything out of life for yourself?' he asked gently.

'Well, I tried that, didn't I? And look what a mess I made of it. I guess you can't force life to give you what you want, you have to make the best of the chances it offers. And you're Nikki's best chance.'

Still he didn't say anything and she hurried on, 'Look, I know I'm older than you—'

'Not that much. Three years is nothing.'

'I was only going to say that I wouldn't embarrass you by falling in love with you, or anything silly.'

'Yes, that would be silly, I suppose,' he said wryly.

'It would be nonsense for both of us, wouldn't it? I suppose we're agreed about that. Look at it any way you like, I *am* older than you and it would be positively undignified. I just want you to be easy in your mind, because I'll never embarrass you that way.'

'You're quite certain, I gather,' he said with a little smile.

'Totally, absolutely certain. It's a promise. And, of course, I wouldn't expect you to fall in love with me. I know you're still in love with Alex.'

'How do you know that?' he asked quickly.

'Because while you were delirious you mentioned her name, several times.'

'While I was speaking in Italian?'

'Yes, so I didn't understand anything you said.'

She reckoned heaven would forgive her the lie. The truth would create an awkwardness that would be a barrier between them for ever.

'I just heard her name,' she persisted, 'and it was very obvious that—well—'

'Laura—'

'You can't marry her, but later you might meet someone you really wanted to marry, and we could get a divorce. So you wouldn't be trapped for ever.'

He stared at her, then rubbed his eyes.

'I'm getting lost here. Wouldn't a divorce make the whole thing pointless?'

'No, because you'd only divorce me, not Nikki. When we were married she could take your name so that she'd feel she was your daughter, which is what she wants. And then she'd always be yours. You wouldn't desert her as Steve did, so even if we divorced she'd still have a father.'

'Good grief, Laura!' he protested. 'We haven't agreed ? e marriage yet and you're already planning our div. Have you chosen my next wife as well?'

'I know it may sound a little strange,' she said hurriedly.

'*A little*—?'

'But I want you to understand that I'd do all I could to make it easy on you.'

'But like I said before, everyone gains—except you.'

'But I would gain, don't you see? If Nikki has a father who isn't ashamed of her, that'll mean all the world to her and that would mean all the world to me. Not gain? I'd gain everything I want.'

He was silent a moment.

'What about Steve?' he asked at last.

'Who's Steve? He's over. He doesn't matter.'

'And suppose there's no divorce and I insist on staying married to you for years? That's your whole life taken up; many years ahead, and Nikki will have gone out into the world.'

'But how she faces the world will be decided now, and that's where you come in.' She gave a light laugh. 'And if I'm stuck with you for years, well, I'll just have to put up with it.'

'Me and my bad temper—'

'Yeah, right.'

'I may go out chasing women every night.'

'You're welcome, as long as you're there when Nikki comes in from school. And if you want to be away overnight that's fine too, as long as we agree a good cover story to tell her, and—'

'Laura, for pity's sake!' he exclaimed, half laughing, half annoyed. 'A nice idea you have of me!'

'No, I think only the best of you, but I want you to know that there are no chains.'

'But if I'm taking on the responsibility of a wife and

child, then perhaps there should be a few chains?' he asked quietly.

'You're right,' she said with a sigh. 'Of course there'd be chains, whatever I said. I was deluding myself and trying to delude you. Oh, Gino, what was I thinking of? Please forget I said anything. It's time I was on my way.'

'Not so fast,' he said, holding onto her hand so that she couldn't move. 'You haven't had my answer yet.'

'There's no need for an answer,' she said hurriedly, 'because I've withdrawn the question. In fact, I never asked it.'

'That's a pity, because I was going to say yes.'

'Look, I'd better—what did you say?'

Gino spoke in a voice that was suddenly firm. 'I said yes. I think we should get married as soon as possible.'

CHAPTER EIGHT

GINO was home three days later. They had waited until then to tell Nikki, and when the moment came they did so quietly, almost casually, not suggesting that they were in love, but concentrating on her.

Her reaction was all they had hoped.

'You're really going to be my daddy?' she asked Gino, eyes shining. 'Honestly?'

'Honestly,' he assured her.

Anxiety tinged her voice. 'You won't go away?'

'No,' he said, understanding at once. 'I won't go away.'

They set the date three weeks ahead at the local Register Office. The boarding-house family would be the only guests, and Nikki would be the bridesmaid. They spent a happy day together going around the shops, buying Laura's wedding outfit, a pale ivory dress that would be useful later. With it she wore a flowered hat, while Nikki had a smaller, matching one that shielded her forehead and made her blissfully happy.

'It's going to be the best day ever,' Nikki said.

Gino looked at her, his head on one side.

'You know,' he said in a considering voice, 'people seeing us together, might think we were really father and daughter. We look fairly alike. Our hair is the same colour. And our eyes.'

Nikki placed herself right in front of him, regarding him steadily.

'We're not really alike, though, are we?' she asked.

Laura's eyes filled with tears. There was no doubting Nikki's meaning. She was reminding Gino of her damaged face, standing where he couldn't help but see it, seriously advising him to think what he was taking on.

She was nine years old.

Gino knew when words were useless. Brushing back the hair from the child's forehead, he drew her to him and laid his lips against the swelling.

'I think we look exactly alike,' he said, 'and if anyone thinks you're my daughter, I'll be honoured.'

Laura saw the look that came into the child's face, and she knew that she was doing the right thing in this marriage.

There was another reason, but one that she wasn't ready to face yet. The knowledge had come upon her suddenly and without warning, disconcerting and almost scaring her. She still needed to discover what she thought about it, and that was hard with Gino constantly around. There was no chance to stand back and consider when events were moving them closer every day.

A visit to a second-hand furniture shop produced a single bed that they pushed into Laura's room to stand alongside hers, and a narrow wardrobe that they only just managed to get into the room.

'Your things don't take up very much space,' Laura said, almost in dismay.

He shrugged. 'I travel light, but don't worry. I'll buy a decent suit for the wedding. And there's something else we ought to talk about.'

A hesitancy, almost an embarrassment in his voice made her look at him quickly, wondering what could follow.

'I thought we'd covered everything,' she said, trying to sound casual.

'We haven't discussed the help I'll be giving you with this place. There must be all sorts of jobs I can do, and we must work out what they are. Cooking for instance. You know I'm good at that. I can do the evening meal, and if you insist on still working at the pub I can do breakfast next day, so you can sleep in a bit. We should draw up a roster—is something the matter?'

'No,' she said quickly, hoping there wasn't a note of hysteria in her voice.

'Then why are you laughing?'

'It's the thought of you, drawing up a roster! I didn't know you were so organised. The state of your room—'

'Never mind that,' he said hastily. 'Just because I'm untidy doesn't mean I'm not organised.'

'Doesn't it?' she asked innocently.

'It'll be better if we make a plan,' he said, grinning in reluctant acknowledgement. 'All right, you make the plan, I'll just follow it.'

'It's a lovely idea, Gino, but are you sure you want to?'

'I'm not just going to be the lodger any more,' he reminded her quietly.

'Then I'll be very glad.'

And that, she thought wryly, would teach her to have unrealistic hopes.

But she cherished their moment of shared humour. It would make the future possible.

Before they left the room she said, 'What about your family in Italy? Will they be coming?'

'No,' he said briefly. 'Now, come and let me show you how well I can cook eggs and bacon.'

He was gone, hurrying downstairs before she could ask any more questions.

On the appointed day they all went to the Register

Office. A brief, dry legal ceremony, and Laura and Gino were husband and wife.

Sadie had a digital camera, courtesy of Compulor, and when they were outside she took picture after picture in various combinations: the bride and groom together, trying not to look too self-conscious; then the two of them with Nikki, standing just in front, beaming with joy; then Nikki and her new father, holding hands, smiling at each other. Looking at those pictures later, Laura knew that the huge gamble she'd taken was worth it.

How different from her first wedding day, when she'd worn a glamorous gown of satin and lace, the reception had been a huge affair at an expensive London hotel, and the guests had been show-business friends.

Now they returned to the boarding house to cut the wedding cake that had been Claudia's gift, while Sadie busily downloaded pictures and printed them out as her gift. The happy couple were toasted in champagne, a gift from Mrs Baxter, who had returned with good news of her grandchild.

On that first wedding day the bride and groom had flown to the Caribbean for two weeks. Laura had been deliriously in love with a man who adored her. Their honeymoon lovemaking had been golden, ecstatic, and the future had stretched out, glittering with infinite promise.

Laura's second wedding day ended with her going to work behind the bar, after which her new husband collected her and they walked home quietly together. He made her a cup of tea and they talked for a while about nothing much. Finally they looked in on their sleeping daughter, and went to their room.

There they lay down in their separate beds and each lay alone, staring into the darkness.

After a while Gino raised himself on his elbow and listened until he was sure Laura was sleeping. He got out of bed and went to sit by the window, looking out onto the dark street, and beyond it the park where his life had changed for ever.

He'd done it, he thought, with wry self-mockery. Gino, the playboy who'd always loved lightly, except once, to whom life was a laugh, had made a sensible, arranged marriage, because now that was the only kind of marriage he could make.

He knew he'd surprised Laura by agreeing so readily, but her suggestion had found an echo in his own thoughts. She'd made it easy for him, laying out the terms methodically, saying in every way but words that she was still in love with Steve Deyton, and that he, Gino, was second-best.

His passionate love for Alex, and its brutal ending, had left him in a desert. He must find a purpose for his life, or live in that desert for ever. Love was over, but there was still the warm affection he felt for Laura, and the knowledge that to Nikki he was a blessing. That would have to be enough. He would make it enough.

'And that's me set for life,' he thought with a faint smile. 'Next stop, middle age. Tomorrow I'll buy a pipe and slippers.'

He stayed by the window until the first light of dawn began creeping through the streets. Then he dropped a light kiss on his wife's forehead, being careful not to wake her, and got into bed.

Laura lay without moving, alert behind her closed eyelids, as she had been all night. She had known the moment when Gino went to the window. She had sensed every move he made, practically every breath he drew.

To the last moment she'd clung to the hope that he would take her into his arms and say to hell with their agreement, this was their wedding night and he was going to make love to her.

But when he merely kissed her and turned away she took a long slow breath and told herself to be sensible. She had been sensible for years now, but suddenly it was very hard.

To Nikki's joy, the circus came to town. Claudia and Sadie astonished everyone by revealing that they were circus nuts.

'But only if there are no performing animals,' Claudia said gravely. 'That we couldn't countenance.'

'But we're assured that there are only acrobats and clowns,' Sadie chimed in. 'And we wondered if Nikki would like to come with us.'

Nikki nodded vigorously, and the visit was planned for a Saturday evening. Mrs Baxter was away, staying with her son to help out with the new baby. Bert and Fred had gone out to a football match that would probably end in an evening out with 'the lads'. So once the trio had left for the circus the house was much quieter than usual.

Laura was looking forward to a meal alone with Gino, and when the phone rang she crossed her fingers, hoping that it was nothing important.

'I'll get it,' Gino said, going out into the hall. 'Hello?'

'Is Laura there?'

'Who wants her?'

'It's Mark.'

He'd been meaning to ask Laura about the mysterious 'Mark' who called her up out of the blue and for whom she would dash off at a moment's notice. But the pressure of events had driven it out of his mind, until now.

'Can you tell me what it's about?' he asked.

'I really need to talk to her urgently. Is she there?'

'I'll fetch her,' Gino said through gritted teeth. 'By the way, you're talking to her husband.'

Laura was already emerging from the kitchen, her eyebrows raised in a query.

'It's Mark,' Gino said, adding with heavy significance, 'he needs to talk to you urgently.'

She whisked the phone out of his hand. 'Hello, Mark?—what's all the panic?' There was a pause during which Gino didn't even pretend he wasn't listening. 'Tonight? Can't you get anyone else?—All right, I'll do it. Where do I go?—Is that all the info you can give me?—exactly how sexy?—black lace, OK. I'll see you there.'

She made some notes, and hung up to find Gino regarding her wryly.

'I know this is an unusual marriage,' he said, speaking lightly, 'but it's still a little soon for you to be dating other men, isn't it?'

'I'm not dating anyone.'

'Well, pardon me for being cynical, *Signora Farnese*, but when my wife arranges to meet another man and asks how sexy he wants her to be, then my antenna begins to twitch.'

'It's perfectly innocent.'

'*Black lace?* Tell me about it.'

His grim tone, so different from anything she'd heard from Gino before, annoyed her enough to make her say, 'I don't see why I should. We had an agreement—'

'It didn't include you making a fool of me. If it's so innocent, why the secrecy?'

'Because you'll make a big fuss about it.'

'I'll make an even bigger one if you don't tell me.'

Laura sighed and gave up. 'It's just a way of earning a little extra money.'

'Oh, this I have to hear!'

'It's very little different to working in a pub.'

'Except that you have to conceal it from your husband.'

'I wish you'd stop calling yourself my husband,' she said crossly.

'Well, I'm sure we dropped into the Register Office for some reason. Remind me what it was.'

'Very funny! Look, Mark is an old friend from my dancing days. Now he runs a little agency, organising party entertainment.'

Laura hesitated, realising that the next bit might be rather difficult.

'Don't stop,' Gino encouraged.

'I deliver good-luck telegrams, birthday greetings that sort of thing. It's a kind of practical joke because I pretend to be something else—a policewoman, coming to make an arrest, something like that. And then, just when the 'victim' is getting agitated, you reveal the truth.'

'Where does the sexy bit come in?' Gino asked remorselessly.

'Well, of course you have to take off the uniform, and show that you're wearing something pretty underneath.'

'You mean *strip* off the uniform, don't you?' he demanded in mounting outrage. 'You're a stripogram girl, aren't you?'

'That's one way of putting it—'

'Do you end up wearing anything at all?'

'Of course I do. It's not a striptease.'

He gave a grim laugh. 'You'll have to forgive me if the distinction is lost on me.'

'I undress down to satin and lace underwear.'

'*Black* lace, I gather?' he demanded ironically.

'In this case, yes.'

'And other times?'

'It depends what the occasion demands.'

'And does Mark turn up with your costume?'

'Only the outer costume—policewoman, traffic warden, soldier, that sort of thing. But I have my own underwear. I keep several items so that I'm ready for anything.'

'Would you care to rephrase that?' he asked dangerously.

'I meant ready for any occasion. As underwear goes it's really quite proper, and I don't show all that much.'

'Laura, how can you be so naïve? You're going to stand in the middle of a crowd of men and remove your clothes, and you say it's not a striptease. What do you think a striptease is?'

'A stripper takes off far more than I do, and ends up almost naked.'

Gino tore his hair. 'You don't know how men's minds work. What matters isn't what you're left wearing, but what you're *seen* taking off. Just watching it removed is—exciting. It's meant to be.'

'You speak as an expert of strip joints, I take it?'

'Don't try to turn this around on me. Just watch my lips. I don't want my wife taking off her clothes in front of other men.'

'Oh, nonsense! I've been doing it for two years.'

'How come nobody knew?'

'I don't do it often. Once a month, maybe twice. It makes a bit of extra money, and I never came to any harm.'

'You weren't married to me then, and don't tell me that you're not because in the eyes of the world, you are. I am an Italian, not a milky Englishman. I don't say, ''Yes dear, no dear, expose your body if you want to, dear.'' I say that what you propose to do is an *infamia*, and I won't allow it.'

He was as close to angry as she had ever seen him. His dark eyes glowed with a light that was almost fierce, and his mouth was set in stubborn lines.

'Don't tell me what you will and won't allow,' she said, incensed. 'This isn't the nineteenth century.'

'I want you to stop,' he said very deliberately. 'Do you understand that?'

'All right, I won't do it again after tonight.'

'You won't do it tonight.'

'Yes, I will, because I've given my word and that's that. I'll tell Mark this is the last time, but I won't let him down.'

Gino glared directly into her eyes. Laura glared back. She'd been her own woman for too long now to take kindly to high-handedness, even from Gino.

At last he turned away sharply, muttering something in Italian that sounded like swearing, and walked out of the front door.

'Damn!' she muttered. 'Damn! Damn!'

After a moment she looked out into the street. There was no sign of Gino, but instinct took her across the road in the direction of the park.

As she'd hoped, he was there, on the same bench as the day they'd met. He was sitting with his hands

clasped between his knees, glowering at the ground. He
glanced up at her approach, and then away again.

'Go away,' he growled as she sat down beside him.
'Let a man sulk in peace.'

How like him, she thought, to diffuse it with a joke.
To think she'd been hoping for a little jealousy.

'No, you never sulk,' she said. 'I've never known you
to get mad before.'

'I've never known you to be stupid before.'

'I told you, this will be the last. That's a promise.'

'And that's supposed to make me feel better?'

'I'm only delivering a birthday card.'

'With you as the birthday gift? Gift-wrapped, *ready
to be unwrapped*?'

'The main part is the joke where I tell him he's under
arrest—'

'No, the main part is where you take your clothes off
in front of a crowd of slavering men. *Mio Dio!* To think
the English are supposed to be a cool, calm race! You
don't go tonight.'

'I do.'

'You do *not*. What do you take me for? You think
I'll just sit back and let you leave the house, knowing
where you're going and why?'

'I haven't asked you to *let* me do anything,' she
seethed. 'Even if we were really married I wouldn't ask
your permission. But we're not married. It's an arrange-
ment, that's all. And you're breaching the terms.'

'I don't recall any terms that cover this situation.'

'Complete freedom,' she reminded him. 'Do what
you want, go where you want, have girlfriends and stay
out all night if you want.'

'And when have you seen me going out with anyone

else, or being out all night? Have I used any of that freedom?'

'No, but—well—you could.'

'When I do, *then* you can lecture me. Until then, don't.'

'Fine. I won't lecture you, and you won't give me orders.'

'The hell I won't!'

'Is this the way you carry on in Italy? Like you're out of the Dark Ages?'

'No decent Italian wife would even think of doing such a thing—'

'Then it's lucky I'm not an Italian wife.'

'Since that day in the Register Office, you *are* an Italian wife, and you'll please behave like one.'

Laura breathed hard. 'I haven't time to argue about this. I've got to get ready.'

Jumping up, she stormed away across the park, listening for the sound of Gino running after her. But it didn't come.

Male pride, she thought bitterly. Plus a lot of shouting and thumping his chest like a gorilla. And what did it amount to? Nothing.

Once back in her room she went to the drawer where she kept her costumes for these occasions, and began turfing out the contents, muttering to herself, 'Black lace with black satin or black lace with red satin? Red, I think. And suspenders with black stockings, plus black lace gloves.'

From down below came the sound she had been waiting for, a door slamming, followed by feet taking the stairs two at a time.

The feet paused outside the bedroom door, as though their owner wasn't quite as sure of himself as he wanted her to believe. But then the door opened. He came in, shut it behind him and leaned back against it, glowering.

'Are those your working clothes?' he asked scathingly, indicating the apparel laid out over the bed.

'Yes. I'm preparing for my farewell performance. It'll be exactly the same as all the others I've done—'

'Oh, no it won't, because I shall be there, watching every move you make.'

'Meaning you don't trust me?'

'Meaning I don't trust *them*.'

'Gino, I don't think it's a good idea—'

'I didn't ask what you thought. I told you what I was going to do.'

Laura stared at him, wondering if this overbearing man rapping out orders could be the same sweet-tempered pussy-cat she thought she knew.

One thing was growing clearer by the minute. The pussy-cat was actually a tiger, and from now on she needed to be careful.

'You have a simple choice,' he went on. 'I'll drive you to this place, and be there to drive you home. You'll introduce me to Mark, and I'll tell him that it stops here.'

'I'm perfectly capable of telling him myself.'

'I'm not sure you'd make it quite convincing enough. The way I'll tell him, he'll believe it. Now, we can do it my way, or we can just cancel the whole evening. Unless you think you can get past me.'

She couldn't fool herself about that. A twenty-ton tank couldn't have gotten past Gino in this mood.

'In that case,' she said, 'I'm going to have a bath, and get ready.'

When she emerged from the bathroom an hour later

she found Gino still in their room. He regarded her with a raised eyebrow.

'Out,' she said firmly, pointing at the door. 'I'm going to get dressed.'

He shrugged and left. Laura prepared herself with great care, knowing that she must maintain a fine balance. She had her job to do, and she owed it to Mark to do it properly. He was a good friend who'd come to her aid with these jobs when money was very tight.

But she must also think of Gino, whose outrage hadn't abated, although he now disguised it with an ironic demeanour.

He'd said, 'I am an *Italian*, not a milky Englishman,' and she was beginning to understand what that meant. There was a dark, brilliant edge to him, almost a hint of danger, that warned her not to provoke him further.

Over a pair of black lacy panties she slipped on the red satin basque, whose bust was wired to push up her bosom, emphasising its fullness. It was laced up in the front, the edges not meeting, but leaving an inch of skin showing. Then she smoothed the sheer black stockings up her legs, fastening them with suspenders.

She made up her face with delicate precision; just enough, not too much. Finally she slipped on a cotton dress over her erotic finery, and covered that with a coat.

Gino was waiting for her downstairs, and together they went out to the car.

'Where are we heading?' he asked.

'The Angel's Head. It's a pub on the other side of town.'

His hackles rose as soon as he saw the place, which was down at heel. From inside came the sound of noisy male singing. Laura thought wryly that perhaps, after all, she was glad Gino was here.

Mark was waiting for them just outside the door. He was a tall, middle-aged man with a fussy manner. Gino relaxed a little, but his greeting to Mark was reserved.

'Mark, this is my husband,' Laura said.

'Well, well, I didn't know you'd got married.'

'But you'll understand why my wife will not be appearing again after tonight,' Gino said quietly.

'Ah, well, that would be a pity. I've got several things lined up—'

Gino's voice was like an arctic fog.

'You'll have to find somebody else. My wife's decision is final.'

'But surely—'

'Final,' Gino said, and something about that one soft word stopped Mark in his tracks.

'Is anyone else coming?' Laura asked Mark.

'No, I'm playing the man, tonight,' he said, then, in answer to Gino's sharp glance he added quickly, 'I just provide the background and play the music.' He held up a cassette player placatingly.

'OK,' Gino said briefly.

Inside the pub she went to the cloakroom and put on the policewoman's uniform that Mark had given her. It was specially designed to be removed easily, being fastened with Velcro.

As a final touch she pushed up her hair beneath the hat to make herself look severe. Now she was ready.

She found Mark waiting for her, also dressed in a police uniform. Gino had vanished.

'Thank goodness for that!' Mark said fervently. 'He's really scary. So, you won't be doing this any more after tonight.'

'That's what Gino says but—'

'No, it's what I say too. I'm not ready to die. You didn't see how he was looking at me. He's not a gangster, is he?'

'Of course not.'

'Well, he's possessed by the devil.'

'Oh, nonsense, he—' she faded into silence.

Mark was right. Gino wasn't Gino any more. He was someone else, a man filled with suppressed fury.

'Here's your notebook, with your words,' Mark muttered.

A young man came towards them. 'Ready?' he said. 'Henry Rufford is the fellow in the red shirt.'

'Here we go,' Mark muttered.

Assuming stern frowns they pushed through the crowd, which fell silent at the sight of their uniforms, and took up position in front of a large man in a red shirt.

'Henry Rufford?' Mark demanded.

'Yes.' The man looked nervous.

'Is that your vehicle outside?'

'Yes—yes, but—'

'Are you aware that it's been reported stolen?'

'But it can't—'

'Officer, read him the report.'

He produced a small cassette radio from under his coat, while Laura began to read from the notebook in a fierce, official voice.

'Henry Rufford, it is here reported that on the twentieth day of August you did reach the age of fifty-five years, and that in consequence your friends have clubbed together to wish you *Happy Birthday!*'

Rufford burst out into relieved laughter. Mark hit a button, making music come from the cassette player, and Laura went into action.

With a swift movement she whipped off the jacket, revealing the top of the red satin basque. An appreciative roar went up from the watching men. Then the skirt came off, revealing the rest of the basque, fringed with black lace, and stockings.

She began to sway with the music, smiling at the audience but always keeping her distance. Gradually she began easing the gloves down her arms, and the roars grew.

The sound startled her. Removing a glove was innocent enough, surely?

Just watching it removed is exciting. That was what Gino had said.

She started on the other glove, sliding it down inch by inch. Henry Rufford leapt to his feet and planted himself in front of her, ogling her bosom with eyes that were practically on stalks.

What happened next was too fast for him to follow. The punch that connected with his chin came out of nowhere, knocking him off his feet. As he sprawled on the floor the contents of a beer mug were deposited over him, and a coldly furious voice in his ear said, 'You're lucky to be alive.'

'Gino—' Laura started to protest.

'*Silenzio,*' he snapped, rising to confront her. 'You leave this place.'

'Look—'

'No, you look. I tried doing it your way. Now we do it my way.'

Before she realised what he meant to do Gino lifted her off her feet. The next moment he was storming out of the building with Laura tossed over his shoulder like a sack of potatoes.

CHAPTER NINE

'JUST what do you think you're doing?' Laura demanded crossly as they emerged into the street. She was struggling to free herself but Gino's arm across her back was immovable.

'What I should have done earlier,' he said.

'There's no need for you to act like a caveman. Will you please put me down?'

'Sure. We're here now.'

He'd reached the car. Opening the rear door he set her down, keeping hold of her and silently indicating for her to get in. It would have given Laura great pleasure to refuse but she couldn't risk a scene in the street, especially dressed as she was. So she climbed into the back of the car and sat, seething in silence, as they drove home.

To her relief the house was dark and empty.

'I think we should go upstairs,' she said grimly when the front door had closed behind them. 'There are things to be said.'

'There certainly are,' he agreed, indicating the stairs with an ironic gesture. 'After you, my lady.'

The events of the evening must have affected her, for she was uncomfortably aware that her scantily clad behind was right in his sights as they climbed the stairs. Or perhaps it was something new about Gino himself that made her intensely conscious of her own body.

When they were safely in the bedroom she rounded

on him. 'You've got a nerve, Gino, acting like that, showing me up—'

'You were making a pretty good job of that yourself.'

'I told you what would happen—'

'You told me you could cope.'

'So I could.'

'Rufford was trying to grope you up,' he shouted.

'I could have handled him.'

'That's what he wanted,' Gino said crudely.

'To think I used to believe you were a civilised man.'

'No, I'm an Italian. It's not the same. I have my own notions of "civilised", and they don't include standing by while my wife strips for other men. And don't hand me that line about how innocent it is because *I saw their eyes.*'

He was breathing hard. 'Every man there wanted to tear the last piece of clothing off you, and it wouldn't have been difficult.'

'It would have been impossible because I wouldn't have allowed it,' she said hotly.

'You think you'd have had any say? It would be easy to pull open that bow at the front—like this.'

With one swift movement he proved his point. Just one little tug at the satin strings that tied the basque in the front, and the knot slid undone. Another tug at the strings and the whole lace-up down the front was loosened.

Laura stared down at herself, then up at him. Her heart beat faster at something she saw in his eyes. He was watching her, trying to read her expression.

'You see how easy it is?' he asked softly. 'You were never as safe as you thought in this flimsy thing. It only needs one man without any manners.'

As he spoke he was twining his fingers in the strings,

easing them open, widening the gap so that the two sides fell further apart, revealing her waist and her breasts.

A pulse in her throat was making it hard to speak, but she managed to say, 'I've never before met a man without any manners.'

'You have now,' he said, his eyes on her breasts.

Now he was pulling the string out, letting it slither through the holes, so that the basque fell further and further apart until it was completely released, and he tossed it aside.

His next act took her by surprise. Placing his hands on her waist he lifted her up high, as easily as if she weighed nothing.

As he lowered her gently he drew her closer, so that his face fitted naturally between her breasts. At once Laura forgot all notion of quarrelling with him. Who needed it? Overwhelmed, she took his head between her hands, pressing his face against her, feeling his mouth against her flesh.

The sensation was so good that she let out a long sigh of satisfaction. This felt right and she was ready to give herself over to it totally.

She could feel Gino shaking as he lowered her slowly to the ground and began raining fierce kisses on her neck, her throat. He kissed like a man who'd restrained himself for too long and wouldn't be denied now. His mouth moved over hers with purpose, coaxing and demanding at the same time, in a way that deeply excited her.

She pressed closer to him, offering her own mouth to his, answering his desire with ardour of her own. She'd thought passion was dead in her. Instead it had been banked down, waiting for the touch that would ignite it and bring it to new heights.

He lowered her quickly onto the bed and began to strip the clothes from his tall, lean body. Seeing him naked, Laura realised that his shoulders were broader than she had thought, the thighs more powerful, deepening her impression that this was a man she'd never really known.

He was ready for her, his urgency unmistakeable. The sight made her heart thump faster as she thought of what must happen soon.

But at that moment Gino stopped as though an arresting hand had been put on his shoulder. Instead of lying on the bed beside her he sat down, breathing hard but in control of himself. Laura saw the sudden question in his eyes, and understood it.

She answered it silently, reaching up her hand, grasping his and pulling him closer to her. His face relaxed.

'Are you sure?' he whispered.

'Quite, quite sure.'

She was on fire, half wild from the need to have him touch her, and when he did so, just lightly with his fingertips, she reacted so swiftly that she startled herself.

The heat seemed to stream through her, bringing a pink flush to her skin, making her breasts grow firm and peaked. She was embarrassed to have revealed so much about her own need. She'd been wanting exactly this for some time, and now he would suspect.

But such practical thoughts were swallowed up in the rising tide of sensuality that was blotting out the rest of the world. All her perception was narrowing down to this one moment, this one man, who was caressing her with skilled hands.

He'd drawn back, wanting to be certain she was willing, but now nothing could have held him. His body pressed her down against the bed while his mouth covered hers. His tongue flickered against the inside, causing a sigh of pleasure to break from her.

She pressed back against him, her arms wrapped around his neck, while she could feel him trying to touch her everywhere, rousing her until she was impatient for him. The moment when he plunged into her felt like the culmination of her entire life.

She seized him, drawing him in, driving against him, relishing his power and her own, inciting him on to claim her more and more completely.

This answered all questions. How long had she secretly wanted Gino in her bed? Since that first day on the park bench when she'd admired him as a healthy, beautiful animal?

What had really prompted her to propose to him? She'd hidden the truth from herself, but now it was fighting its way to the surface. She was seized up in the fierce rhythm of desire, moving faster with him until there was nowhere else to go but into the glittering void.

In the moments when reality returned they discovered that they were still clinging on to each other, as though for safety. As they drew apart she could read her own astonishment reflected in his face.

'I had no idea,' she murmured.

'Nor had I until recently.'

He threw himself onto his back, gasping, but still holding onto her hand while he recovered. Then he propped himself up and looked at her naked body, pale and mysterious in the dim light.

'You've been holding out on me,' he said wryly.

'I have? How?'

'Those prim and proper clothes you wear—'

'Plain and dowdy, you mean?'

'Some of them, almost like you were doing it on purpose.'

'That's how I saw my life,' she admitted, breathing slowly to steady herself against the turmoil that was only gradually subsiding. 'I suppose I dressed for the part.'

'You fooled me—for a while. There were a few hints, like when you brightened up for Steve. Then nothing—until tonight.'

He looked down at her and ran one hand over the length of her body. 'I should have remembered that you'd been a dancer,' he said. 'You move like a dancer, graceful in everything. And tonight, you knew just what to do and how to do it. And those few extra pounds you told me about.' He laid a hand on her hip. 'Just there, enough to make you nicely curved. And here—' His fingers drifted over her breasts, sending a little shiver through her.

'I suspected,' he mused, 'but I didn't know for sure until I saw you putting it on display for other men. And—I minded.'

Gino knew his words didn't express one tenth of what had been happening inside him, but he couldn't have found the right words. If there were any. He wasn't an analytical man. He lived through feelings, not thoughts, and he'd been shying away from feelings, which added to his confusion.

Since he'd left Italy he'd lived like a monk, from choice. The passing fancies he might once have enjoyed were barred to him by his sense of despair and isolation. At times he'd wondered if he would ever seriously desire a woman again.

His friendship with Laura had been sweet to him, but

things had happened that had taken him by surprise. After her first date with Steve she'd returned home, radiant. He'd held her in his arms and wanted to kiss her, and known that he must not. He'd seen her safely and chastely to bed, but nothing had been quite the same after that.

There was something else, to do with the time when he was delirious, but that mystery had yet to be explained. What was no longer a mystery was his own reaction to Mark's telephone call: furious physical jealousy, that had grown worse every moment as he'd stood in the crowd watching her remove her clothes.

It was, as she'd claimed, a fairly modest strip. But it hadn't seemed so to a man whose desire for her had caught him suddenly, almost unaware, and was rising by the minute. Every flash of those long, lovely legs, every wriggle of her hips had tortured him, until he snapped.

'Yes,' he repeated. 'I minded, more than you'll ever know.'

She gave a chuckle that sent a frisson of pleasure up his spine. 'I reckon I do know now,' she mused.

'Just don't forget it.'

'I didn't recognise you, the way you've been acting.'

'I didn't recognise myself.'

'Poor Mark. He thought you were a gangster.'

'Let him go on thinking it. He'll be safer that way.'

'Gino, you don't really mean that.'

He looked at her in an odd way, and did not answer directly. 'Let's just say that I'm naturally possessive,' he said. 'You're mine. No argument.'

'Who's arguing?'

He was silent for a moment, his face clouded.

'Maybe I have no right to ask,' he said at last, 'but—you and Steve—?'

'No,' she said at once. 'I never slept with Steve.'

Compared to this wild, physical craving, how restrained had been her feelings for Steve; not love or passion so much as the need to ease her loneliness and have some kind of future.

'I'm glad,' Gino said. He began to run his hands over her again.

To Laura it was thrilling and satisfying to know that she could rouse him to powerful sexual jealousy. It was only a fraction of what she wanted from him, but she couldn't think of that now that his touch was causing the tide of excitement to rise in her again. For a while there would be nothing else but desire, and craving for the satisfaction that only he could give her.

He let his fingers drift down over her breasts to where the nipples were peaked.

'Mine,' he murmured again. 'And here—' his hand moved down to her waist '—and here—' his fingers found the tops of her thighs, then eased their way gently in to the place that was now home. *'Mine.'*

'If that's what you want,' she murmured, trying to think through the forks of pleasure that were invading her where he touched.

'Yes,' he whispered against her mouth. 'That's what I want.'

One easy movement brought him over her and then he was inside her again, moving more slowly than before, prolonging the pleasure, bringing skill to the service of strength. Now she discovered him as a subtle, generous lover, as well as a powerful one, seeking to learn the caresses that brought her delight, and offering them gladly.

She tried to hold back on her climax, wanting to prolong everything until the final moment, but at last she yielded to it and felt again the joy and profound fulfilment she'd known before.

When he rolled onto his back she propped herself up and, watching him, wondering why he was grinning.

'What is it?' she asked, giving him a gentle poke.

'I was remembering some thoughts I had recently, about heading for middle age. I even planned to buy a pipe and slippers.'

She gave a crack of laughter and buried her face in the pillow to muffle the sound.

'Middle-aged,' she gasped. 'There's nothing middle-aged about you, *signore*.'

'I'm glad you think so, *signora*.' He added wickedly, 'Of course it's different for you, so many years older than me—'

'Ah, yes,' she said with a melancholy sigh. 'That's going to be a big problem soon, isn't it? I should have remembered.'

'Hey, don't be like that,' he said, instantly concerned. 'I was only joking.'

'I know,' she said sadly, 'but it's just that—oh, well, I'll get used to it.'

'But I didn't mean it that way,' he said desperately. 'Laura, please don't be hurt—'

She raised her head to look at him, her face brimful of laughter. 'I'm not,' she chuckled. 'Ever been had?'

'Why you—!' He pulled her into his arms, laughing. 'You wait,' he threatened. 'I'll get my own back.'

'Is that a promise?'

'That's a promise?'

'Now?'

'Think I can't?'

'Well, you've done all right so far—for a middle-aged man. But three times in one night is a bit much to—'

Her words were cut off by his mouth on hers. Gino had never been a man to duck a challenge and he threw himself into this one with all his heart and all his considerable strength. Their two previous encounters had only taken the edge off his desire, not satisfied it completely.

This mating was vigorous, unsubtle and joyful, leaving them both gasping and drained, clasping each other until the last moment, unwilling to let it go. But when it had finally slipped away, Gino fell asleep at once, and Laura found herself mysteriously alone again.

It shouldn't have happened after their closeness, she thought with a little ache. For a while they had been as united as any two people ever were on earth. And yet, as she watched his sleeping face, she saw that he was still, in many essential respects, a stranger.

She had never really known him, except for the glimpse of the truth she'd had in the hospital, when he'd held her hands and poured out his heart to another woman. Tonight one part of him had reached out to her, but she knew the essential part was as far away as ever.

They had lived in the same house for months, shared jokes, confided troubles—or at least, she had confided hers. But in all that time she'd known only what he wanted her to know. Tonight the mask had slipped, or he'd chosen to discard it, and she'd met a man who was moody, unpredictable and dangerously sexy. She could hardly believe that she'd ever thought of him as a brother.

She leaned over and kissed him so gently that he didn't wake. Snuggling down to sleep, she reflected that this was only the beginning. He wouldn't always turn away from her. Now that they had started to find each other there was much more to hope for.

On the surface nothing had changed. To the world they presented the appearance of a sedate married couple, working hard at their jobs and their stolid, virtuous family life.

But behind their closed door life had changed completely, being neither sedate nor stolid. And if they were virtuous, it was only in the sense that, as a married couple, their fevered couplings were, as Gino hilariously put it, sanctioned by law.

There was almost as much humour as sensuality in their lovemaking. Laura would cherish for ever the moment when the two single beds slid apart, causing Gino to fall off her and down the gap. He had climbed out, cursing horribly, and resumed his occupation almost without a pause.

After that they bought a double bed.

Nikki was still their priority. Gino was the father Laura had hoped he would be, and if she had any doubt that he made the child happy those doubts were set to rest one evening in an unexpected way.

It was a Saturday, they had the house to themselves, and Nikki was allowed to stay up an extra hour. They were watching television, channel hopping, when suddenly Laura heard a voice she had thought she would never hear again.

'Of course the people have changed, but the audiences—'

It was like listening to a ghost to hear Jack Gray's voice again. Since the day he'd left her they'd talked only twice, on the telephone. The divorce had been conducted through letters and lawyers.

Now there he was on the screen, still handsome in a lardy way, a few years older and more bloated. His teeth were too large, white and even, as though he'd had them 'done'.

It was too late to switch channels. Nikki, sitting on the floor, had already seen him and was watching the screen intently. When the commentator gave his name Gino looked at Nikki, then at Laura, who nodded in despair.

Since the night Nikki had passionately insisted that her father was dead, there had been no more mention of him. She seemed to have forgotten all about it, and Laura hadn't dared to raise the subject, fearing to upset her again.

But the programme made it clear that he was alive now. Laura snatched up the television guide and discovered that this was a programme about theatrical agents, especially those who were becoming well known.

Now they were talking about Jack's new wife and toddler. He was sitting there with a little girl on his knees, a perfect, beautiful child.

Laura held her breath as Nikki watched the pictures flashing across the screen, underlying the full scope of her father's betrayal. It was almost eerie the way Nikki didn't react.

But then she did react, so subtly that it would have been easy to miss. It was the slightest movement, shifting across the floor in Gino's direction, so that she was leaning against him. He reached down, she clasped his hand in hers, and they sat like that for a moment, until Nikki looked up.

'Can I have some toast before I go to bed?'

'Want me to make it for you?'

'Yes, please, Daddy.'

That was all it took, and all it needed.

Laura would have been happy now if only she could have felt free to tell Gino that she loved him. At night they lay in each other's arms, exchanging warmth and pleasure. By day he treated her with affection.

But he never told her that he loved her.

She reasoned with herself that his behaviour implied love, but she knew better. He was a warm-hearted man whose sweet temper and sensual gifts would have won over any woman. He gave her what he could of himself, and if he could not give more, she knew the reason.

She tried not to brood, knowing how quickly that could destroy her and everything she'd won. But at night she listened jealously to hear if he talked in his sleep, and which name he spoke. He never did utter the name she feared, but neither did he utter hers.

He would never really be hers, she thought wistfully, not in the way that she had become his. She must try to be content with what she had.

One evening he went out, saying that he was taking a walk, although it was raining heavily. He was gone for many hours, returning, very wet, when Laura had already gone to bed, past one in the morning.

'I'm sorry if I disturbed you,' he told her, sitting on the edge of the bed and rubbing his hair.

She didn't tell him that she'd been lying anxiously awake. She didn't want him to feel spied on.

'Shall I get you a hot drink?' she asked pleasantly.

'No, thanks. I never catch cold. Laura, I want you to leave the pub. You do too much.'

'But the money's so useful.'

'There's another way to get money, enough for you to stop being a barmaid, and hire people to help with this place.'

'That sounds expensive. Where can we get enough to do that?'

'I'm going to sell my half of Belluna.'

She sat up. 'Your farm in Tuscany?'

'Half mine. Rinaldo owns the other half and I think he'll be glad to buy my share from me. It'll make all the difference to us.'

'Do you think you'll get very much for it?'

He told her how much Belluna was worth.

'How much?' she gasped. 'But I never dreamed—I always thought you were as poor as a church mouse.'

'So I am, until I sell up.'

'But can he raise that kind of money? Don't farmers have it all ploughed into the earth?'

'True, but Alex can raise it. She had a London apartment that she must have sold by now. If they buy me out that'll put a line under everything, and I need not go back there ever again.'

'Is that what you want Gino—to be cut off from your home for ever?'

He hesitated for the briefest moment before saying, 'This is my home now.'

'That's a nice thing to say, but I don't think it's completely true. Tuscany is where you were born and raised, your language, your culture, everything. Part of you is always going to belong there.'

He sighed and didn't deny it. 'Just the same,' he said, 'it's best if I don't go back.'

She knew she should stop here. She could feel him

withdrawing from her as she grew dangerously close to his secret self. But she couldn't make herself stop.

'Why?' she persisted. 'What is it back there that you can't face?'

'Does it matter?'

'It matters to me. Oh, Gino, you'll never know how much it matters. Tell me.'

'I can't,' he said sharply. 'I don't know the answer myself.'

'I think you do.'

Gino looked at her, and for the first time his face was completely closed against her.

'I'd rather we left this,' he said in a hard voice that contained a warning.

'But I can't leave it. It's too important.'

When he didn't speak she persisted, 'Why Gino? Why can't you go back? *What are you afraid of?*'

CHAPTER TEN

'WHAT are you afraid of?'

The words seemed to glitter in the air, like knives, flashing between them.

Laura regretted them the moment they were out, but it was too late. Gino rose and threw her a look of bitter reproach.

'Why do you do this?' he asked. 'Why do you threaten what we have with meaningless fears?'

'How can they be meaningless when you're afraid too?'

'Laura, for both our sakes, be quiet. There are things it is better not to say. I have made my life here with you and Nikki. It's a good life. I'm happier than I ever thought I'd be again.'

'Yes, happi*er*. That's not the same as happy.'

'I can't make these fine distinctions.'

'But you know what I mean.'

'Yes, I do, and I beg you to say no more.'

'And if I stay quiet, will that change anything? Will the truth you fear go away?'

'There are some questions I don't want to ask, not because I'm afraid of the answers, but because there may not be any answers. I want to protect what we have. For pity's sake, don't make it hard for me to do that.'

Suddenly her eyes were filled with tears. 'I don't know what we have,' she said huskily. 'But if we quarrel, we won't have it any more. Can't you see that?'

She waited, tense and hopeful for his reply. But none came. After looking at her for a long moment he turned and walked out and she heard him going downstairs.

Why couldn't I be sensible? she raged inwardly. *Why can't I leave it there as he wants? We've been granted so much more than I hoped for. Why don't I treasure that without demanding even more?*

Because a love on those terms is no love at all, her heart answered. It's a patchwork love, a make over and mend, artificially constructed from second-hand bits and pieces. And it's not enough.

Gino didn't come back to bed all that night. It was the first time since their marriage that they hadn't slept in the same room.

Next day he greeted her with a kiss and a smile, but he didn't say any more about selling the farm. Laura would have given anything to understand his thoughts. Perhaps she should be glad that he planned to turn his back on Italy and throw in his lot permanently with her in England.

If only she could convince herself that it was that simple!

One day he said to her, 'Have you given in your notice at The Running Sheep?'

'No, you never mentioned it again. I wondered if you'd thought better of it.'

'I haven't changed my mind. I want you to tell them that you're leaving. I've written to Rinaldo saying that I want to sell. He should get the letter about now, and he'll probably telephone.'

After that whenever the phone rang Laura jumped, but the days passed with no call. Gino never spoke of it, or what might be going on inside him, but Laura could sense a rising tension in him, that filled her with foreboding.

When the answer did come it was not a phone call but a letter.

It fell onto the mat in the morning, when Gino was out at work, and she was alone in the house. Laura picked it up, trying to control the sudden racing of her pulse as she saw the Italian stamp.

She couldn't tell whether the writing belonged to a man or a woman. Had Alex herself written to him?

Laura put the letter on the mantelpiece and tried to forget it. But that was impossible, and she kept returning for another look.

Gino telephoned in the afternoon, as he sometimes did, asking whether there was anything she wanted him to bring from the supermarket near the factory.

'There's a letter from Italy,' she said.

She would have given anything to see his face during the long silence that followed. At last he said, 'Fine, I'll see you soon.'

She gave him the letter as soon as he returned home, and watched him grow pale as he read it.

'What is it?' she asked in alarm. 'Does he refuse?'

'It's not from Rinaldo,' Gino said slowly. 'It's from Alex.'

'What does she say?' Laura asked, trying to speak normally.

'She says Rinaldo can't afford to buy me out, but she can, with the money from the sale of her London apartment. She'd buy it in her own name. But first of all she wants to meet us and talk about it.'

'Us?'

'She wants me to take you, and Nikki, to Tuscany. She says it's time we met as a family. She's mad at me for not bringing you before, or inviting them to our wedding. I suppose she's right.'

'Gino, have you only just told them that you're married?' she asked, astounded.

He nodded.

'You quarrelled with them as badly as that?'

'It wasn't a quarrel—not exactly. It was just that we couldn't be close any more. I needed the distance.'

'Do you still need it?'

'I think it's time to do as she suggests,' he said, not answering directly. 'The sooner we go the better.'

'All of us?'

'All of us, including Nikki. Do you both have passports?'

'Yes, but—'

'But what?'

For some reason Laura took fright. 'But I can't come. Who'll run this place?'

'I think our friends will find a way to get by for a while,' Gino said.

He was right. The five tenants rose up in outrage at the notion that they would be helpless without her, and Laura found herself with no way to back out.

Nikki was over the moon at the thought of going to Italy, and soon had the journey by heart.

'We take the plane to Pisa Airport,' she recited, 'because that's the nearest airport to Florence, and then we get the train—'

'I think someone will meet us,' Gino said, smiling at her. 'I've still got to check final arrangements.'

He called Italy that evening, and Laura heard him say, *'E, Rinaldo.'*

'Daddy's talking to his brother,' Nikki told her in a stage whisper.

'I know that, and stop earwigging,' Laura said firmly. 'It's none of our business.'

'Doesn't matter anyway, they're talking Tuscan dialect.'

'How do you know?'

'Daddy taught me some Tuscan words. Only I don't know enough to follow what he's saying,' Nikki sighed regretfully.

'So I should hope. Behave yourself!'

'Oh, Mummy, isn't it exciting? Daddy's told me so much about Italy.'

Gino came off the phone.

'I've booked the plane tickets,' he said. 'We fly the day after tomorrow. Someone will meet us and drive us to the farm.'

'Someone?'

'I don't know who it will be,' he said quickly. 'It's harvest time, so nothing's certain.' Turning his attention to Nikki, he said, 'So get packing. *Capisci?*' Understand?

'Capisco!' Nikki saluted and raced off.

The child's excitement got them through the time, filling in the gaps that yawned because they didn't know what to say to each other.

The whole house was in cheerful uproar. Everyone seemed to be personally delighted at the trip. Sadie went out of her way to arrange Gino's time off at work.

'The job's there if he wants it again,' she said, adding, 'although I don't suppose he will.'

'I suppose when he's sold his share of the farm he won't need to work as a packer,' Laura reflected.

'That's not exactly what I—oh, well, have a good trip.'

When Sadie had gone Nikki said melodramatically, 'They're hoping we don't come back.'

'Darling, whatever do you mean?'

'I heard them talking. They've got it all planned. If you stay in Italy they want to club together and buy this place, because they like living here.'

'You're making that up.'

'No, honestly. They want to have a commune.'

'Now I *know* you're making it up.'

'It's what Claudia said. She's dead keen.'

'Yes, Claudia, forming a commune with Bert! If you'll believe that, you'll believe anything. They can't stand each other.'

'I think that's mostly for show. They'd miss their spats if they lost them. They're all dead keen to buy you out.'

'But darling that isn't going to happen. Gino's selling his share of the farm and coming back here.'

'Does Poppa really want to do that?'

'Poppa? Since when did you call him that?'

'That's what Italian children say. It's what he called his father. He told me.'

Nikki skipped away, leaving Laura feeling disturbed. The decision was made, surely? Gino was turning his back on Italy and returning to spend the rest of his life in England. And yet from every side there was pressure for a different decision. Nikki was becoming determinedly Italian. And if she were right, the problem about the guest house seemed to have solved itself naturally. It was almost as if she were being guided somewhere, by Fate.

But then she remembered Alex and the fantasy fell apart. If there was one thing that Fate would not, *could* not, do to her, it was to send her to live close to Alex,

Gino's true love, and the woman for whom he pined in his heart.

Why, oh why, she wondered, had she insisted on him going back to Tuscany? She was deeply regretting it now.

But then she remembered that it would have made no difference what she said. Gino was going back because Alex had said so, not herself.

Everyone came out to see them off, standing on the pavement and waving madly until the taxi was out of sight. And they did look like a family, Laura had to admit.

The rain was teeming down, but no rain could quench Nikki. For the whole of the journey to the airport she bounced with excitement and bombarded 'Poppa' with questions, sometimes in reasonable, if basic, Italian. Young as she was, she was rapidly becoming bilingual.

The reason wasn't far to seek, Laura thought. Nikki learned because her heart was in it.

She had flown before, but so young that she couldn't remember. Now she enjoyed everything about the airport except for one moment when a couple of boys in their early teens glanced at her face and giggled.

Instantly Gino planted himself in front of them. 'If you have some comment about my daughter, you can make it to me,' he said with deadly quiet.

They paled, then took to their heels.

'Come on,' Gino said, his hand on her shoulder. 'Let's get out of here to a country where the sun shines.'

On the plane Nikki glued herself to the window, regarding the land below with fascination. It had turned into a beautiful day, with little cloud, and she could tell the exact moment when they passed over the coast of France.

'Have we reached Italy yet?' she demanded every five minutes.

'No, that's still France,' Gino told her. 'Then it's Switzerland, and when you see mountains down there you'll know it's the Alps, and we've nearly reached Italy.'

'And then we're there?'

'After a few more hundred miles, *si*,' he said, grinning.

He ordered some champagne and clinked glasses with Laura. The atmosphere was cheerful, and their first trip abroad together might almost have been their honeymoon.

Briefly she regretted persuading Gino to marry her. She was in love with him, and every day it grew more important to know the truth about his feelings for her. Yet because of the way their marriage had come about, she might never know.

'Daddy is that the Alps?'

'Si, piccina. Sono le alpi!'

Soon after that they began to descend, swinging out over the sea before coming in to land at Pisa, near the coast.

From the moment they left the plane Gino felt as though he was watching a tape being replayed. It was harvest, the golden time of year, when the farmer could look at his crops and know how he would prosper in the year ahead.

Last year they had made a mistake, harvesting the grapes too soon because Rinaldo had wanted the money early to repay the mortgage that Alex held. That way he would be free to love her, without the shadow of commerce hanging over his motives. So he'd reckoned.

But he'd got it wrong, harvesting the grapes too early

because his mind had been on Alex. At the harvest festival they'd found each other. In the same moment Gino had lost them both.

And now it was harvest again, and it was time for the circle to be completed.

'Someone's trying to get your attention,' Laura said, pointing.

It was Toni, the foreman at Belluna, a huge, grinning man.

'Don't worry about Nikki,' Gino said softly to Laura. 'I told Rinaldo, and he'll have warned everyone.'

Toni greeted Gino with a bellow, enfolding him in tree-trunk arms, greeting 'Signora Farnese' deferentially, and offering his hand to *la piccina*.

Soon their luggage had been piled into the car and they were turning out of the airport, heading north. Nikki, sitting in the back with her mother, gazed eagerly out of the window. Laura had expected the two men in the front to talk in Italian or Tuscan, but after a few early remarks nothing was said. Gino too was looking out of the window, and Laura could only guess his thoughts as familiar scenery came into view.

Once he glanced over his shoulder to say, 'This is Belluna now, that you can see all around you.'

She saw rising terraces of vines, with men and women picking grapes vigorously. The sun was warm and brilliant on the vivid colours, reminding her how Gino hated the English rain. How could he have borne to leave this place? she wondered.

'There's the farmhouse,' Gino said at last.

At first Laura couldn't believe what she was seeing. The building was pink and almost palatial, with two shallow staircases curving up the front.

'That's a farmhouse?' she asked, dazed.

'It is now,' he said. 'It was a great house, many years ago. There is Teresa, in the upper window.'

An elderly woman was leaning out to wave, then disappearing. As the car drew up outside the house a man appeared at the top of one of the staircases, and stood watching them.

This had to be Gino's brother, Laura thought, seeing the resemblance. Rinaldo was older, heavier, but they clearly came from the same family.

He came slowly down the steps and paused at the bottom, regarding the brother he hadn't seen for a year. Gino gazed back, and Laura had the strangest sensation that neither of them knew what to do. Then Rinaldo opened his arms and Gino went into them. They held each other for a long time in an embrace that spoke of a closeness deeper than any estrangement.

Rinaldo held his brother at arm's length, considering him.

'You're older,' he said in English.

'You're not,' Gino said.

Rinaldo nodded and a slow smile came over his face, as if he were saying that happiness was the reason for his improved looks. It seemed to Laura that he could imply his happiness, but not put it into words, even with his brother.

'You have kept a secret from us,' Rinaldo said, still in English, indicating Laura. 'You should not have done so. Such happiness should be shared. *Signora*, I salute you. You are welcome to our family.'

He kissed her on both cheeks.

'Thank you,' she said. 'I'm really glad to meet Gino's family.'

Gino had moved to stand behind Nikki. 'And this is my new daughter,' he said. *'La mia figlia.'*

Rinaldo and Nikki shook hands.

'*Buongiorno, signore,*' Nikki said.

'She's been practising her Italian,' Gino said proudly.

'So I see.' Rinaldo thought for a moment before asking, '*Come sta?*' How are you?

'*Molto bene, grazie,*' Nikki returned at once. Fine, thank you.

Rinaldo grinned his approval. 'Your daughter is a credit to you, *signora,*' he said. 'Come inside and meet my wife.'

Now that the moment was here Laura tried to stay calm, but she was filled with tension at the thought of the coming meeting between Gino and Alex.

Rinaldo led the way into the house, not back up the stairs but through a French window on ground-floor level. The room ran right through the house, and at the far end was another French window, through which a woman was walking.

At first Laura could see her only in silhouette. After the first glance she looked away, in Gino's direction and saw him stop, a look of astonishment on his face as the woman came into clearer view.

'Alex?' he whispered.

'You see, you're not the only one who's been keeping a secret,' Rinaldo observed, smiling. 'Congratulate us. Our baby is due next month.'

Seemingly in a daze, Gino approached the heavily pregnant woman, and took her hands.

'Gino, dear, you're going to be an uncle,' she said, smiling into his face. 'We're both so glad you came home in time.'

'Rinaldo was right,' Gino said. 'Secrets should be shared with families. Especially wonderful secrets. I'm very happy for both of you.'

He kissed her cheek and led her forward.

'Alex, I want you to meet my wife, Laura.'

The two women shook hands, each regarding the other with deep interest, and each recognising the interest of the other.

'Rinaldo and I were so glad when we heard that Gino was married,' Alex said. 'We know you're going to make him very happy.'

Laura said something polite, but she was trying to equate this calm woman with her inner vision. Gino had said she was an accountant who had lived in London, and Laura had built up a picture of cool, precise elegance, ultra-professional, ultra-chic, composed. The person she'd seen in the picture had been chic even when enjoying herself at a street festival.

But this Alex was somebody else. Her fair hair, falling to her shoulders, looked as though she'd dragged a comb through it at the last moment. And her loose floaty garments weren't just the result of her pregnancy. She somehow conveyed the impression that they represented the person she was.

She kissed Laura warmly. 'Let me take you up to your room,' she said. 'I've put you in Gino's old room, and Nikki is in the one next door.'

She took the child's hand and indicated for Laura to come upstairs with her. The house was beautiful, old and homely and lived in. Nikki clearly thought so too, because she was looking around her, smiling and nodding her head.

Behind them came the men, carrying the heavier suitcases. Laura noticed how Rinaldo positioned himself just behind his wife on the stairs, and kept anxious eyes on her.

Gino's old room was large, with a low ceiling, and

heavy exposed beams. The furniture was deep, burnished walnut, polished until it gleamed.

'Oh, look, Mummy,' Nikki breathed at the window. 'Look at the view!'

The house stood on a small incline, with a view right across a shallow valley. The valley was an almost enchanted place, with pine trees, grass and a stream wandering through it, shining in the sun.

'What's that over there?' Nikki asked, pointing at a building standing on the far side, a little way up the facing incline.

'It's a house,' Alex said.

'Who lives there?'

'Nobody. Rinaldo has offered it to people who work on the farm. It's big enough to take two families. But it's supposed to be haunted and nobody will touch it.'

'Haunted? You mean a real ghost?' Nikki demanded, wide-eyed.

'That's what they say,' Alex said, amused. 'But I don't know if anyone's actually seen it.'

'Can I go and look some day? I'm sure I'd see it.'

Laura sighed. 'I'm afraid Nikki's a real little ghoul.'

In Nikki's room they found a welcome gift, a huge jigsaw puzzle of the Ponte Vecchio bridge over the River Arno.

'We'll go there and see it soon,' Alex promised her. 'Come down as soon as you've finished unpacking, and we'll have something to eat.'

Rinaldo was waiting for her in the doorway. Laura, returning to her own room, saw him draw Alex's arm through his as they went down the stairs.

'He really fusses over her,' Laura said, going into her room.

When there was no answer she looked up and found

Gino staring out of the window at the golden landscape. He seemed transfixed.

Quietly Laura came to stand beside him. He neither moved nor spoke, but she could sense feelings of satisfaction, almost of joy, coming from him as he looked out at his home once more.

'It's not raining here,' she said softly.

'No,' he said. 'It does rain sometimes, but not—it's different.' He seemed to come out of a dream. 'I'm sorry, what were you saying?'

'About Rinaldo and the way he fusses over Alex. You wouldn't think it at first. He looks one of the strong, silent types.'

'I suppose he is,' Gino said. 'But he lost his first wife when she gave birth. It always haunted him, and I suppose now more than ever.'

Downstairs they met the housekeeper Teresa, an elderly woman, and the two maids, powerfully built young females called Claudia and Franca, whom Gino told her were Teresa's great-nieces.

The meal was a banquet. The table had been decorated with flowers and candles, and the fare was a celebration of Tuscan cooking. First there was *finocchiona*, salami flavoured with fennel seeds, then black cabbage soup, followed by stuffed pheasants with cream and truffles. To finish there were sorbets, or fruits in syrup, with ice cream.

Rinaldo sat at one end of the table with Laura on his right. Alex sat on her other side. Rinaldo sometimes engaged her in courteous conversation, but mostly he left the talking to his wife. If Laura happened to glance at him she always found his eyes on Alex, anxiously brooding.

To Laura's relief, the three servants all spoke English,

even if a fairly basic kind. Rinaldo explained how Alex had won Teresa's heart by alerting him to the fact that she was getting old and needed help in the house.

'For her sake Teresa started to learn English,' he said fondly, 'and she also made Claudia and Franca learn it, on pain of a terrible fate.'

Nikki had made instant friends with the maids, practising her Italian, which was getting better by the day, and teaching them new English words. When it was time for her to go to bed the three of them went upstairs in a companionable threesome.

The others went out onto the patio to drink coffee. It was dark now, and after a while they began to see moving lights between the trees.

'Our friends are coming to welcome you,' Rinaldo said.

'You told everyone we were coming?' Gino asked.

'We told nobody, but you know this district.'

As he spoke he rose to his feet to greet their first guests. After that someone arrived every few minutes, until Laura reckoned there must be almost two hundred people.

They all greeted her with a kindness that didn't disguise their curiosity. It was clear that the word had gone around the district that Gino had returned, bringing a wife with him, and nobody wanted to miss it.

But hand in hand with the curiosity was an unmistakable warmth. She was welcome. They knew nothing about her, but she was welcome.

And when Nikki, attracted by the noise, crept down the stairs and hovered in the doorway, there was a roar of greeting for her, and nobody was startled or disconcerted by her appearance. Like Gino, they seemed oblivious.

She began to understand her husband better that night. The warmth in his nature was his own, but it was also a reflection of the people from whom he came. He had said, 'I'm an *Italian*, not a milky Englishman,' and she'd thought she knew what he meant. Now she realised that it meant much more.

Smiling, she turned to look at him, wanting to tell him what she had discovered.

But he wasn't there. After looking around for a while Laura saw him sitting in a corner with Alex, his head bent close to hear what she was saying. He looked completely absorbed, as though he'd forgotten everyone else in the world.

CHAPTER ELEVEN

NOBODY seemed to have any sense of urgency about arranging the sale. Rinaldo said that Gino must inspect the farm closely before they could make any decisions. For several days they went out together, driving across the land, coming back late.

This threw Alex and Laura together. The first time he saw them getting into the car Rinaldo detained them, anxiously enquiring of Laura whether she could drive.

'Yes, I've been driving a car for years,' she assured him.

'Rinaldo, stop worrying Laura,' Alex chided him. 'I'm doing the driving.'

'But if anything should happen—'

'I'm not due for another three weeks.'

He scowled at his wife. It was clear to Laura that he demanded his own way, and disliked all opposition, even from the wife he was supposed to love so much.

'You might get tired,' he growled.

'Then I can drive,' Laura said.

He turned his glare on her. 'But here we drive on the other side of the road. You're not used to that—'

'On the farm it doesn't matter,' Alex said. 'There's no right and left on our roads. *Amor mio*, please stop fretting. All is well.'

Rinaldo sighed and gave in with a poor grace. 'You've got your mobile phone?' he demanded.

'Yes.'

'And you know the number of mine if anything happens?'

'I've known your number for a year,' she reminded him with a touch of wifely exasperation.

'But does Laura have my number?'

'Give it to me,' Laura said, whipping out a pencil and notebook, and writing it down as he recited it.

'There now, I've got your number,' she said. 'And I've got Gino's number, and he's got my number.'

'And I've got Alex's number,' Gino said. He'd wandered up to see what was keeping his brother. 'And she's got my number, and Nikki has everybody's number.'

Everyone except Rinaldo laughed at this.

'OK, OK,' he said, 'I know you think I act like a crazy man.'

Alex touched his face. 'It's all right. Don't worry.'

He made a noise that sounded like a growl, and stepped back from the car, letting Alex start up. Laura smiled as she waved goodbye to Gino, trying to tell herself not to mind about what she had just heard.

What did it matter that Gino and Alex had exchanged private phone numbers, and she hadn't known about it?

On that first day the two women and Nikki went to see the 'haunted' house. It was about a hundred years old, a great barn of a place, but solidly made.

'Does it really have a ghost?' Laura asked.

'A woman murdered her faithless lover here years ago,' Alex said. 'Now she's supposed to wander for ever, wailing. If she exists, I feel sure Nikki will find her.'

But Nikki had nothing to report, even seeming to feel cheated. She managed to convey the impression that in a well-ordered house there would have been a ghost.

'But even without a ghost, it's a lovely place,' Alex pointed out. 'Of course, it needs some work. There's no electricity or running water, but that's easy to arrange. And when it's been redecorated, just think how it would look.'

Laura said nothing. A chill fear was gathering in her stomach, spreading out to encompass all of her. Alex was telling her that she and Gino could return to the farm and live here.

Obviously that was her plan. Rinaldo seemed to be a disagreeable man, and perhaps her marriage to him had disappointed her. Now she regretted driving Gino away, and was tempting him back.

Laura pulled herself together, telling herself to be sensible. But how often had she already told herself this in the short time since she'd been here? Too often. Last night Alex and Gino had been absorbed in each other's company, today there had been the hint of secret conversations.

Well, what else had she expected? She'd always known the truth.

On the second day Nikki went with Rinaldo and Gino to watch the gathering of the harvest. Alex took Laura into Florence.

'I have to go first to see my employer,' she said.

'Your employer?'

'I can't just be a farmer's wife. I was an accountant in England, and now I'm learning Italian accountancy in the office of a man called Tomaso Andansio. Sometimes he gives me things to take home and work on. Today I have some files to return to him.'

She stopped at a set of offices in the Via Bonifacio Lupi, and introduced Laura to Signor Andansio as 'my sister-in-law'.

She was treated as an honoured guest, offered coffee and cakes while Alex was going over the files she'd brought with her boss. Then Signor Andansio himself showed her around the building, which was a place of great historical interest. It was an enjoyable visit.

But as she was returning to the office where Alex worked, she saw, through the open door, Alex answer her mobile with the soft words, *'Ciao, Gino.'*

Then her host drew her attention to a picture on the wall, and she heard no more of the conversation until Signor Andansio turned away for a moment, and a few words reached Laura clearly.

'No, I haven't said anything yet—I have to wait for the right moment—no, *caro*, I want to explain this to her myself—promise that you will leave it to me.'

She hung up. When Laura entered the office a few moments later nobody could have told her inner misery from her smile.

Mercifully there was no need for private conversation as they had lunch with some friends of Alex's. It extended deep into the afternoon, so there was only the journey home to get through, and they managed that by discussing the lunch.

At home Nikki was waiting with an eager account of her day. Laura listened attentively, trying not to watch Gino and Alex to see if they were talking. She saw nothing that would have aroused her suspicions normally, but these conditions weren't normal.

For the first time she knew the bitter destructiveness of jealousy, and wished she could be anywhere in the world but here.

Alex was obviously tired, and as soon as the meal was over Rinaldo suggested that she go to bed, in a peremptory way that was almost an order. She smiled and agreed.

Laura also chose an early night, bidding the brothers goodnight and leaving them together while she went up with Nikki. When she had seen the little girl to bed she returned to her own room and sat by her window, wondering what had happened to her life.

Down below she could hear Gino and Rinaldo talking in Tuscan, their voices sounding contented.

Does Rinaldo know? she wondered. *Does he suspect? Is that why he's so ill-tempered?*

After a while the voices stopped and she heard them come upstairs. A click of the latch and Gino was there with her.

'You're not in bed yet,' he said.

'No, I waited up. I was watching the night. It's different from England, so much blacker and more velvety.'

He was pulling off his clothes.

'You're right. It's beautiful, isn't it? Have you ever seen anywhere as lovely as Tuscany?'

'No,' she said quietly. She was sick at heart.

He'd stripped naked now, and slipped his arms about her.

'I'm glad you're still up,' he said, nuzzling her neck.

'I waited because I wanted to talk to you,' she said, trying not to respond to the excitement he could create in her so easily.

'What is there to talk about?'

'How can you ask?' she said. 'We came here for a reason—to sell the farm.'

'Mm!' he said against her hair.

'You've been talking to your brother for days.

Haven't you—decided anything yet?' It was hard to talk
while he was touching her purposefully.

'It's not easy to value the place until the harvest is
in,' he murmured. 'We shall have to stay a little longer
for that. I thought you liked Belluna.'

'It's a beautiful place but—Gino, please—I must ask
you—'

'Not now,' he murmured against her neck. 'I've been
thinking of this all day.'

Of this, she noted. Not of her.

'Gino—'

'Hush, kiss me—kiss me—'

She should be strong and refuse, but his lips were
already against hers and she was kissing him whether
she meant to or not.

She felt her nightdress slip to the floor and then he
was taking her to bed and making love to her with a
vigorous ardour that left her no chance to think, or to
be aware of anything but the shattering sensation of
having him inside her, driving her on to more and more
pleasure.

It was only afterwards, when he was deeply asleep
on the other side of the bed, and she lay alone and sad,
that she wondered whether not giving her a chance to
think had been the idea all along.

Laura dreaded the next day when she must smile and
talk and try to seem normal, but in the event she was
allowed a little merciful solitude. Rinaldo and Gino
went to Florence. Alex rested, and Nikki joined her new
friends in the kitchen, learning to cook.

Laura took the car that had been placed at her dis-
posal, and drove out to explore the landscape. By a

stream she stopped and got out to walk, hoping that her mind might become clearer.

By the time she returned to the vehicle she had recovered her courage. What did they think she was, to sit idly by while they decided her fate and informed her at 'the right moment'? Was she supposed to be such a fool that a little cynical lovemaking could silence her fears?

She drove back to the house. Rinaldo's car stood outside, so Gino and Rinaldo must have returned. But when she walked onto the veranda she could see only Gino, sitting with Alex, a grave look on his face.

They both smiled when they saw her, but she could sense their unease.

'I've come to say that I want to go home,' she said simply. 'I need to go back to the guest house, and Nikki must return to school. It's been kind of you to have us—' she nodded to Alex '—but now it's time for us all to leave—if Gino will come with me.'

She thought she heard Alex murmur, 'Oh, no,' as Gino rose to his feet in consternation.

'Laura, please, I beg you abandon this idea. I know you only want to live in England and I'd hoped for more time to explain to you—'

'Perhaps you don't need to explain,' she said, her eyes kindling. Turning to Alex, she said, 'It's no accident that you asked Gino to return, is it? You always meant to keep him here.'

'That's true,' Alex said simply.

Whatever Laura had expected it wasn't such a ready admission. She drew in her breath, bracing herself for the worst while Alex continued speaking.

'As you say, it's no accident. I always meant him to stay, and you, and Nikki. But we knew you'd need a lot of persuading, so we waited, hoping that you'd come to love this country. Perhaps we waited too long. Many times I've wanted to confide in you.'

'Confide what?' Laura asked slowly, for there was a note in Alex's voice that made her wonder.

'That I'm worried about Rinaldo—the baby is due soon—'

'Gino told me about his first wife and child. Is that it?'

'Yes, but there's more,' Alex said earnestly. 'The baby keeps turning and facing the wrong way. The doctors keep turning it back, so that I don't have a breech birth, but then it swings around again. It's no big deal. Lots of women have breech births, but Rinaldo gets anxious.'

There was a fond note in her voice, and a soft tenderness in her eyes.

New understanding came to Laura. 'But it might be a big deal, mightn't it?' she asked.

'Not really. It's just that—well, if something went wrong—oh, Laura I'm so glad you and Gino are here. Rinaldo couldn't bear it if anything happened to me. He's not as tough as he tries to make out, and he depends on me so much. He would need his brother, desperately.'

'Alex, you're not going to die,' Laura said.

'No, I don't believe that I am, but if I did—I dread to think of him left alone.'

She looked up with a frantic appeal in her eyes. Laura's head seemed to be reeling with what she'd heard. Then Alex said something that shocked her.

'And if I weren't here—you could come and live in Italy, couldn't you?'

She gasped. 'Alex, what are you saying?'

'I'm putting it very badly, but I must try to make things right for Rinaldo now in case I can't do it then.'

Before Laura could answer there was the sound of footsteps outside.

'Rinaldo!' Alex said. 'Gino, please—'

He went out and they heard him hailing his brother, then their voices going in the opposite direction.

'Quickly before they come back,' Alex said. 'I wanted to say to you that if anything happens, Rinaldo will need his family. And then—then you wouldn't be afraid of me any more.'

'I'm not afraid of you,' Laura said firmly.

'Aren't you? You don't need to be, you know.'

'I don't know what gave you such ideas—' she said lamely.

'I've seen you watching Gino, wondering. You know our story. Didn't you come here to find out?' Alex sighed. 'Maybe I've been selfish. I was racking my brains for a way to bring Gino home for Rinaldo's sake, but I couldn't do it while there was any chance that he might still have feelings for me. And then his letter came, telling us about you, and I knew everything was all right.'

'You make it sound so simple,' Laura sighed.

'Sometimes it can be.'

'The situation between Gino and me is not simple,' Laura said. 'And since I came here the two of you have seemed to be sharing a secret.'

'But not the secret you thought. I explained everything to him on the first evening. We should have told you then, but we thought you'd refuse if we dumped it on you too soon. I wanted you to fall in love with Tuscany first, so that you'd *want* to stay here.'

Alex gave a little laugh at herself.

'I thought I was being so clever, having it all worked out. But I have no gift for intrigue. I used to have, but that was in the days when figures were my whole life. It's easy to be clever with figures.'

She took Laura's hand in hers.

'You won't tell Rinaldo any of this, will you? It would only worry him more.'

'Not a word,' Laura promised. 'And look, none of this is going to happen. You're going to have that baby, and you'll both be fine.'

'And then you plan to leave? That's what you're telling me, isn't it?'

Laura hesitated. 'I don't know,' she said at last. 'I simply don't know.'

They didn't speak of it again. There was nothing for Laura to do now but bide her time until the child was born. Then she would know, she told herself. But to say that was to ignore all the other times she'd promised herself that she would know at some moment in the future. And still she was uncertain.

She set herself to learn as much as possible about Belluna, its ways and its people. If she must make a decision, at least it would be an informed decision.

Rinaldo still seemed to her a grouchy, ill-tempered, domineering man. But, armed with her new knowledge she could see that he was living on his nerves, and once or twice she caught him regarding his wife with a look of such terrified vulnerability that Laura was pulled up short. But if he noticed anyone observing him the look vanished quickly, to be replaced by a harsh glare.

Alex drove her all over the estate, seeming to understand, without words, her need to know as much as possible. Once she stopped at a small church and led

Laura to a quiet corner of the graveyard, where one stone stood alone. Laura couldn't understand the words, but she read the names,

Maria Farnese, aged twenty-three, and Isabella Farnese, born and died on the same day.

'She was Rinaldo's childhood sweetheart,' Alex said. 'Gino said they were so happy, but they had less than two years together. She died giving birth, and Isabella died within an hour. He still comes here.'

'Do you mind that?' Laura couldn't help asking.

Alex seemed genuinely surprised by the question. 'Of course not. The past is the past. Denying it is as futile as being jealous of it. Rinaldo loves me, and I love him. But she loved him too, and she still does. I come here sometimes to reassure her that I'm taking good care of him.'

'You—?'

Alex looked at Laura's astounded face and burst out laughing.

'It's all right, I'm not crazy, although I suppose I sound like it. If I were still the person I was when I lived in London I'd think I was crazy too. But I'm Italian now and it's different here.'

'How?' Laura asked urgently.

'You feel things in the air. It's something to do with families—they're very strong in Italy, and people go on being family members even after they die. It's almost as though they haven't died at all. I know Maria as if I'd spoken to her. Rinaldo is a sacred trust that she gave me to care for, and one day I'll answer to her for how well I protected our husband.'

The implied words, 'and it might be soon,' hung in the air. But nobody spoke them. Nobody needed to.

As they left the churchyard Alex said cheerfully, 'I gather we're going to have a treat at supper tonight.'

'I hope it turns out to be a treat,' Laura said fervently. 'Nikki really fancies herself as a cook.'

'Don't worry. Teresa will keep a close eye on her, and it'll come out right.'

'I don't even know what she's cooking,' Laura admitted. 'They all closeted themselves in the kitchen this morning, and when I looked in Nikki drove me away and said it was a big secret.'

Alex laughed. 'I can't wait.'

Suddenly she stopped and clutched the nearest headstone, gasping heavily.

'Alex, what is it?'

Alex spoke in a strange voice. 'I think my waters have broken.'

'Yes,' Laura said tensely. 'Then you're going to start contracting soon. Where's the phone? We'll call an ambulance.'

Alex grasped her hand. 'It'll take time for it to get here. Would you mind driving me to the hospital yourself? It's in Florence, near the Via Bonifacio Lupi, where I took you before.'

'All right, let's get you into the car.'

She helped Alex to the vehicle and eased her into the back where she had more room. Then she got behind the wheel, wishing there wasn't so far to drive to Florence.

'Surely it's not due?' she asked over her shoulder as she swung out into the road.

'Not until next week, but I guess the baby's picked its own time,' Alex said with another gasp which escalated into a groan. 'Laura, you had a baby. How long after the waters do the contractions begin?'

'It varies. With some women it's twenty-four hours. With me it was three. But it can be a lot quicker.'

'It couldn't be just a few minutes, could it?'

'Yes,' Laura said frantically. 'I believe it could. Hold on. I'm going as fast as I can. Thank goodness these country roads are clear. I hadn't quite realised what a big place Belluna is.'

Suddenly Alex screamed.

'You can't be having contractions yet,' Laura protested. 'It's much too soon.'

'Would you like to tell the baby that?' Alex demanded with grim irony. *'Oh God!'*

Laura made a desperate decision.

'What are you stopping for?' Alex cried.

'There's still a good hour before we get there. And I don't think we have that long.'

'Are you sure?'

'When I had Nikki something like this happened to the woman in the next bed. She told me her baby had come so fast it was born in the ambulance.'

'You think that's happening?'

'Don't you?'

'Yes!'

Laura jumped out and got into the back. Alex was fumbling for her phone, calling Rinaldo.

'It's happening, *amor mio*. Very quickly. We've stopped the car at—' She described their location, but the words ended in another prolonged gasp. Laura took the phone from her.

'Rinaldo? Listen, stop worrying, Alex is fine. It's happening very fast, so we need an ambulance here quickly. Can you direct them?'

His voice reached her, tense and strained. 'Yes, I know where you are now.'

'Good, I'll hold the fort until they get here.'

Her voice sounded brisker and more authoritative than she felt, but she had to keep everyone calm. That way she just might manage to stay calm herself.

'The ambulance will be here soon,' she told Alex when she'd hung up.

Alex's face was contorted. 'No time—any minute—'

'Please Alex, try to—'

Try to what? Stop the baby being born? It was coming at any moment. They both knew that.

'It's all right,' Alex murmured. 'As long as you're here—'

This was no time to be scared.

'Fine,' Laura said, sounding brisk again. 'And I am here, so it's going to be all right.'

She pulled off her light linen jacket, setting it aside for the baby. Carefully she assisted Alex to lie lengthways along the back seat. Inwardly she prayed for the ambulance to hurry. Outwardly she smiled.

'You won't forget?' Alex murmured. 'If anything happens—'

'Now, that's enough,' Laura interrupted her robustly. 'Nothing's going to happen except that you're going to have a healthy baby, and you're going to have it a lot faster than most mothers do, I promise you. *Ow!*'

The yell was drawn from her by the sudden tightening of Alex's hand on her own, almost crushing her with its power.

'Go with it!' she said, wincing. 'And the next one. Come on—come on—Alex, everything's fine. I can see the head. It's lying the right way round. Not a breech birth.'

Even through the pain that swamped her Alex managed a smile of relief. Ten minutes later the child emerged easily into Laura's hands.

'It's a girl,' she said, wrapping the infant hastily in her linen jacket.

Alex was looking in her baby's face with passionate fondness, but she glanced up at Laura.

'Thank you,' she said. 'Without you—'

Laura found that her eyes were suddenly blurred. She brushed the tears aside, and when she looked up again she could see another car through the rear window.

'It's Rinaldo and Gino,' she said.

She got out and went towards them as Rinaldo slammed on his brakes and leapt out, his face distraught.

'For God's sake!' he shouted.

'No panic! The baby's born safely. Go and see.'

He rushed past her into the car.

'Are you all right?' Gino asked, looking at her anxiously.

'Yes, and Alex is going to be fine when she gets into hospital. It's a girl, perfect as far as I could see.' She gave a slightly hysterical laugh. 'There was no breech birth. Alex was worrying about nothing. So was Rinaldo.'

'Worrying about nothing?' he asked. 'When the birth happened so fast and without warning? Suppose she'd been alone out here when it happened? But for you there might have been a tragedy.'

That startled her.

'Well—yes—I didn't think. Anyway it's all over now.'

He regarded her fondly. 'Is that all you have to say about being a heroine?'

'The most scared heroine in history. I shall be glad when that ambulance—oh, thank goodness, there it is!'

They went to the car, whose door was standing open. Rinaldo was in the back seat with his wife and daughter. His head was bowed over the infant, concealing his face, and it took Laura a moment to realise that he was sobbing violently.

Alex had one arm around her child. The other hand was stroking her husband's head. For just a brief moment she glanced up and her eyes met Laura's, and the two women exchanged a smile of total understanding.

CHAPTER TWELVE

THAT night the family, minus Alex, celebrated with the supper Nikki had prepared. It was pronounced a triumph, and Nikki, fired with culinary genius, began making plans for the welcome home feast for when Alex returned with baby Laura.

There had never been any doubt about the name. The story of the birth had spread all over Belluna and now, wherever she went, she was greeted with cheers, and even applause.

She had become part of Belluna. If everyone's reaction hadn't told her, the naming of her new niece would have done. She had earned their respect, and was no longer an outsider, watching from the sidelines as her fate was decided.

As Alex had always known would happen, Rinaldo's grouchiness vanished when he was no longer afraid for his wife's safety. He doted on his new daughter, and openly treated his sister-in-law as a heroine.

'The men of this family are so soft-hearted,' Alex said to Laura, smiling, one evening when she had put the baby to bed. 'When I was pregnant Rinaldo used to ask me a thousand questions to see if I was all right. You heard him. Now he asks a thousand questions to see if little Laura is all right. I'm really becoming sidelined.'

'Oh, yeah!' Laura said cynically, and Alex laughed. She glowed with the confidence of knowing where she belonged with her child, her man, her place in the world. It was the thing Laura most envied her.

One evening, as they were putting the baby to bed, Laura said, 'Alex, do you realise that you don't need us any more?'

'Whatever do you mean?'

'Everything's going well for you. The harvest was a record, the danger's over—'

It wasn't entirely a surprise when Alex became a little vague and self-conscious.

'Actually—' she began.

Laura smiled. 'Go on.'

'There was a little more to it than that. Even without the baby, Rinaldo and I wanted Gino to come back and see us as we are now, married and loving each other, a true family. Otherwise in his mind we'd have stayed frozen in time, as we were on the day he left, and that would have been bad for him, for all of us.

'Rinaldo needs his brother. Little Laura needs her uncle, and me—well, I suppose I need to know that I didn't do him any permanent harm.

'This last year Rinaldo and I have been so happy, but there's always been a shadow spoiling it, the fear that he might never be happy again.'

She looked hopefully at Laura, who nodded but stayed silent.

'Laura, we so much want you all to stay,' Alex said on a note of pleading. 'Belluna is Gino's home, his birthright. I don't think he can really settle anywhere else. But maybe I'm wrong. I can see he's changed this last year. It's not just that he's older. He's more thoughtful. He's found another life with you, and maybe he doesn't need this one any more.'

'No,' Laura said at once. 'You're not wrong. I've

been thinking the same thing. Before your letter arrived I told him he should come back here. I was so afraid that he'd sell up, then discover too late that it had been a terrible mistake.'

'Ah, you understand him. I thought you would. You wouldn't let him make a really bad mistake.'

'You're very kind,' Laura said wryly, 'but our marriage isn't—as you think. Did he tell you that I proposed to him?'

'No,' Alex said, looking at her strangely. 'I know that Nikki was a part of your decision, but not that you actually made the proposal. But so what?' She gave a very Italian shrug. *Non è importante.*'

'Of course it's important,' Laura said, astonished. 'It's the wrong way around.'

Alex shrugged again. 'Marriages happen as they happen. My own marriage was delayed because Rinaldo wouldn't say he loved me until the harvest was in, and he could pay off the mortgage. Have you ever heard anything so absurd? Then, of course, he got impatient and harvested the grapes too soon, so they weren't worth so much. Honestly, the foolishness of men!'

'But I asked Gino to marry me because Nikki wanted him to be her father.'

'And that's the only reason? You didn't love him? Or have you only come to love him since? You're not going to deny that you do love him, are you?'

'No,' Laura said, smiling and shaking her head. 'Of course I love him. How could any woman help loving him? Oh, sorry—I shouldn't have said that?'

Alex laughed. 'It's all right, I agree with you. I love him dearly. He's very lovable. But it's not the kind of love I share with Rinaldo. That comes from another world. Gino is like my younger brother. In fact, he *is* my younger brother now.'

'That's how I saw him,' Laura mused. 'Or thought I did. But for me it didn't work. I think I was in love with him then, although I didn't know it. By the time I admitted it to myself we were already married, and now I'll never know how he really feels about me.'

'You never talk about it?'

'What is there to talk about?' Laura asked simply. 'If you marry without saying you love each other, the subject somehow never comes up again.'

'And I suppose he didn't tell you what he said in his letter to Rinaldo?'

'No.'

'I think perhaps you ought to know.' Alex reached into a drawer and pulled out a sheet of blue paper, that Laura recognised as her own. But when she held it out Laura shook her head as soon as she saw the words.

'I can't read Italian. And besides—' she struggled with temptation '—should I read Gino's letter if he doesn't want me to?'

'Of course you should,' Alex said robustly. 'I've no patience with that way of thinking. How would the world ever get by if nobody ever did anything they shouldn't? I'll translate for you.'

Laura gave up. In truth she was longing to know what Gino had said about her.

'''Now I have something to tell you,''' Alex read, translating as she went. '''The two of you always said that I would find someone of my own, who would be to me what you are to each other. I didn't believe you, but it's happened. Her name is Laura, and if she knew I'd described her in such a way she'd be surprised, and perhaps angry with me. We married a few weeks ago, and they've been the happiest weeks of my life, even though I know I'm only second-best to her. The fact is that Laura only married me for the sake of her daughter Nikki, a lovely child, who has adopted me as her father. Laura's actually in love with another man, but he insulted Nikki so she turned her back on him, and made do with me instead.''"

Laura turned away to hide the emotion on her face. Even to Alex she could not reveal what it did to her to hear what she meant to Gino like this, at a distance.

Second-best? Made do with him? If only he knew!

Alex was still reading.

'"Bit by bit we're forming what I hope and believe is a happy marriage, although it may be some time before she accepts me completely. I can be patient, however long it takes, for she is worth waiting for. All my life, if necessary.''"

Alex lowered the letter and looked at Laura.

'Is he right?' she asked. 'Are you in love with another man?'

'No, of course not. Steve was just—' Laura made a helpless gesture '—we went out for a while, and I would have married him for security. After he'd gone I found I didn't mind.'

'Did you ever tell Gino that you don't mourn this man?'

'No, we don't talk about feelings. When I proposed I told him he could have all the freedom he wanted, even girlfriends, as long as he was a good father to Nikki.'

'Good heavens!' Alex began to laugh. 'And you're surprised that the poor man is confused? I don't wonder he doesn't discuss feelings with you. You've got him walking on hot coals. He still thinks you're doing everything for your child.

'Mind you,' she added, turning fondly to the cradle, 'I understand that. There's nothing I wouldn't do for this little one. I think Gino would understand as well, because he has a father's heart.'

She gave Laura a special smile. 'Have you told him?'

'I—no. I wasn't sure myself until recently. I'm waiting for the right moment, but I'm not sure when that will ever be. I was hoping for some sign that he loved me—'

'And you think you haven't had it? What do you think that letter was all about?'

'Yes, he implies it in a roundabout sort of way, but he never comes right out and mentions love.'

'Perhaps that's hard for him,' Alex said shrewdly. 'The last time he told a woman he loved her it was here, at Belluna, in front of a crowd. He went down on one knee and told her of his love. And when he'd done that, she rejected him and married his brother.'

'Yes, I know.'

'I should think that declaring love to a woman is the most difficult thing in the world for him, even if he were sure of her feelings. And he isn't sure about yours at all.'

'I should have simply told him,' Laura said, nodding as understanding came to her.

'So, it's time to put it right,' Alex said firmly. 'You'll have to try to forgive me, but I'm going to interfere in your life again. I'm afraid I'm just one of nature's "fixers".'

Laura regarded her sister-in-law and a slow smile spread over her face.

'What did you have in mind?' she asked.

*   *   *

Gino spent the day in Florence attending a meeting of local grape growers. The light was dying as he returned home in the early evening.

'Gino.'

As he entered the house he looked around for Laura, but it was Alex's soft voice that reached him from half-way up the stairs.

'Where's Laura?' he asked.

'I don't know. Will you do me a favour?'

'Of course. Just let me see Laura first.'

'I think she's out.'

'Think? Don't you know? Is she driving around alone? It's getting dark.'

'Look for her later. I need you to go over there,' she pointed to the house facing them on the far side of the valley. 'I was there today and I left my bag. Please Gino.'

He was too good-natured to refuse her, but he would gladly have done without this.

'Fine, I'll go, but I wish I knew where Laura was. I need to talk to her.'

'I can't think why,' Alex said with a touch of irony. 'You never seem to say anything to the purpose.'

Something strange in her manner got through to him.

'Alex, what's going on?'

'Something that should have been "going on" before. You ought to have told Laura long ago that you loved her, but since you lost your nerve I did it for you.'

'You what?'

'I told her how much you loved her. She didn't believe me at first, so I read her your letter.'

'Alex, you wouldn't dare!'

'My dear boy, I'd have done anything to stop you

wandering around, treading on eggshells. Gino, it was all nonsense about that other man. She never loved him. She said so. She said a lot of other things too, but she'll have to tell you herself. I've given you a start. The rest is up to you.'

Gino had come halfway up the stairs to her, his face a mixture of shock and wild hope. Now he turned to descend, then thought better of it and took the last few stairs in a leap.

'Alex,' he said, 'Alex, my dear, dear sister!'

She kissed him. 'Go on with you.'

'But where can I find her?'

'I meant go and get my bag.'

'Yes, right.'

He went back down the stairs and out into the car. Rinaldo, who'd been watching from a doorway, mounted the stairs to his wife, his eyes warm as they rested on her.

'What are you up to?' he asked, suspicious and tender at the same time.

'Up to? I don't know what you mean.'

'I mean that I saw your bag ten minutes ago.'

'Did you?' she said vaguely. 'You must have imagined that.'

'No, I didn't imagine it. And I repeat, *amor mio*, what are you up to?'

Alex smiled.

'I just thought that after what Laura did for us, it's time we did something for her.'

Gino normally regarded himself as a man who was quick on the uptake, but he was within a couple of hundred yards of the house before it dawned on him that he'd been set up.

He stopped the car and sat there quietly, his eyes on the building, rearing up in the fast-gathering gloom. As he watched he saw a small light in one of the windows, as though someone had put on a lamp.

If you were superstitious, you might think that the ghost walked. Or, if you were a man in love, you might think that someone was waiting for you, impatient because you'd taken so long.

For a long time he hadn't thought of himself as being in love with Laura, because their relationship had come about so strangely that they had missed out the romantic, mysterious stage.

Or perhaps he hadn't wanted to admit the truth to himself.

But if you desired a woman so powerfully that her every movement was a delight and you woke up thinking of last night's lovemaking, and spent the rest of the day looking forward to the next night—and if, in addition, you were moved by the longing to take all her troubles from her, so that the knowledge of her defencelessness could make your bones melt in your body—well, did you call that love?

And if, in your stubbornness and pride, and perhaps cowardice, you still refused to call it love, what else could you possibly find to call it?

Suddenly something came back to him: the night he'd returned home to the farm and found Alex in Rinaldo's bed, both of them asleep. Rinaldo had rested against her breast, in the circle of her arms.

In the past Gino had flinched from that picture, but this time he looked at it head-on, and understood its true meaning for the first time.

Rinaldo had lain against her like a man seeking refuge, and there had been protectiveness in the way her arms curved about him, enfolding him in a circle of safety.

Rinaldo, the powerful, the harsh, the dominant, had turned to Alex because she was a strong woman, and offered him a refuge. Beneath the rough outer shell he was defenceless in ways only she had divined.

And he himself—Gino had only just understood— was precisely the opposite. His laughing, easy manner had always fooled people into thinking him boyish and unreliable. But, in truth, he was the stronger man.

Alex's beauty and charisma had caused him misery, but he knew now that he would never have been happy with her. She was too independent to need him as he must be needed if he were to know peace and fulfilment.

But Laura's vulnerability had spoken to him from the first moment, although it had taken time for him to understand. She could be strong and resourceful. The child's birth had proved that. But for her daily life she needed the strength he had to offer, and his heart had chosen her because she called forth the better part of himself. They completed each other, just as Rinaldo and Alex completed each other. There could be no stronger union than that.

The light was still there in the window. Gino started the engine and drove the rest of the way. As he went into the house, he knew what he would find.

'Hello,' she said, smiling at him.

'Hello,' he said, gazing at her.

She was enchanting, her face illuminated by the glow of the lamp. When she put out her hand he took it in his, gently caressing her fingers with this own.

'What is it?' she asked when a sudden alert look came into his face.

He raised her right hand to study the thing that had

caught his attention. It was a small filigree ring on the centre finger.

'Nikki gave me that,' she said. 'She won it at a fair. You've seen it a thousand times before.'

'Yes, but I never realised—'

And suddenly he was back in the hospital, rambling feverishly to the woman who sat with him, speaking in a warm voice, full of hope, saying 'Time to forget and love again.'

He'd denied it, but she'd pleaded, 'Suppose she loved you. Don't you want to *be* loved as well as to give love?'

Then he'd drawn her hand closer and brushed his lips over it, feeling the rough outline of a ring on her finger.

A filigree ring.

'It was you, wasn't it?' he asked now. 'In the hospital, that time.'

'Yes, it was me.'

'Why did you never tell me?'

'I couldn't while you loved Alex so much.'

'I thought I did. But you said such things to me while I was in that fever—about a woman who loved me as much as I loved her. Who did you mean?'

She shook her head. 'You know who I meant.'

'But I need to hear you say it. Tell me that you love me, Laura, please.'

'I love you,' she said simply. 'I have for a long time. I always will.'

'And I knew I loved you soon after we married,' he admitted, 'but I didn't know how much. I had to come back and see Alex again to realise what a small part of my life she was. You *are* my life. My whole life, now and for ever. You and Nikki. The three of us.'

She placed his hand on her stomach. 'Four,' she said.

She put down the lamp quickly to go into his arms, and as they held each other tightly she felt the shadow between them finally pass away.

'There's so much I wanted to say to you,' he said, 'But I could never forget that you only married me for Nikki's sake.'

'I thought I did. I had to tell myself something like that, as a kind of protection. I was scared to admit how much I loved you, even to myself. I couldn't believe that I really meant anything to you.'

He kissed her. 'You were right when you said that I had to come back. You're wiser than I. You knew the past had to be dealt with. Even though I loved you, it wouldn't have been complete without this.'

He took her face between his hands, searching it anxiously. 'What happens now?'

'I called England this afternoon, to tell them they can buy the house. We can use the money to put this house in order.'

'It's all settled, isn't it?'

'It was settled before we arrived. Alex chose this place ages ago, but do you know why? Look.'

She picked up the lamp and went to the window, staring across the valley to where they could see the lights of the house he'd just left. Some of them were on, but there was one darkened room, where he could just see a gleam of light, as though an answering lamp had come on.

'We'll always be within sight of each other,' Laura said. 'When it's dark, we can look out and see their lights, and they can see ours. It had to be here and nowhere else.'

She raised the lamp high, moving it back and forth. As Gino watched, incredulous, the pinpoint of light in the far building, also moved back and forth, as though in answer.

'Who's doing that?' he asked.

'Alex of course,' she said calmly.

'You and Alex—friends?'

'Friends and allies, as sisters ought to be. Look.'

She moved the lamp again, and back through the darkness came the answer, the ancient, unmistakable message, that he'd thought never to find again.

It was the same message that he'd discovered in Laura's arms, in the circle of her love, and it was wonderfully, overwhelmingly right that it should be she who evoked it for him now, shining across the darkened valley.

All's well. Welcome home!

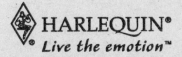

If you enjoyed what you just read,
then we've got an offer you can't resist!

Take 2 bestselling
love stories FREE!
Plus get a FREE surprise gift!

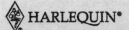

Coming Next Month

#3811 HIS HEIRESS WIFE Margaret Way

Olivia Linfield was the beautiful heiress; Jason Corey was the boy
from the wrong side of the tracks made good. It should have been
the wedding of the decade—except it never took place. Seven years
later Olivia returns to Queensland to discover Jason installed as
estate manager. Should she send him packing…?

The Australians

#3812 THE ENGLISHMAN'S BRIDE Sophie Weston

Sir Philip Hardesty, UN negotiator, is famed for his cool head. But
for the first time in his life this never-ruffled English aristocrat is
getting hot under the collar—over a woman! Kit Romaine, a girl
way below his social class, is not easily impressed. If Philip wants
her, he's going to have to pay!

High Society Brides

#3813 MARRIAGE IN NAME ONLY Barbara McMahon

Wealthy Connor Wolfe has no choice but to marry if he wants to
keep custody of his orphaned niece. Who better as a convenient
wife than his niece's guardian, Jenny Gordon? Jenny agrees—but
secretly she's hoping theirs can be more than a marriage in name
only.…

Contract Brides

#3814 THE HONEYMOON PROPOSAL Hannah Bernard

Joanna has dreamed of marrying Matt from the day they first
kissed—their wedding day, which should have been the happiest
day of her life. But the relationship is a sham, and the marriage
is a fake. So, if it's all pretense, why does it feel so heart-stoppingly
real? And why has Matt proposed a very *real* honeymoon?